HIS ULTIMATE LOVE

Pearl Mampetlana

#THE PAYNE SERIES PLAYLIST

Lloyiso- madoda sabelani

Lloyiso- seasons

Lloyiso-Dream about you

Lloyiso- Nontsikelelo

Little Mix- Love me or Leave me.

Kris Allen- Lost

Ingrid Michaelson- Light me up

Riley Clemmons- Fighting for me

Lloyiso- Intliziyo

Demi Lovato-Body Say

Meghan Trainor- After You

Chord Overstreet- Hold On

Tate McRae- Feel like shit

James Arthur-Train Wreck

Tate McRae-You broke me first

Zoe Wees-Control

Alec Benjamin-Let me down slowly

Ruth B-Dandelions

James Arthur-Say You Won't Let Go

Conor Maynard- What I Put You Through

Slander & Dylan Matthew – Love Is Gone

Dean Lewis-Be Alright

Little Mix- Little Me

Little Mix-No

Little Mix-Think About Us

Little Mix- Enough

Little Mix- Between Us

Elaine- You're the One

Thabsie- Ubuyanini

Yanga- Catch Me

Camille Cabello- Consequences

Rita Ora- Body On Me

Rita Ora- Let You Love Me

Kelly Clarkson- Because of You

Demi Lovato- Tell Me You Love Me

Demi Lovato- Smoke & Mirrors

Demi Lovato- I Hate You, Don't Leave Me

Rihanna- Love On The Brain

Selena Gomez- The Heart Wants What It Wants

Selena Gomez- Good For You

Selena Gomez- Rare

THE PAYNE SERIES

His To Marry

His Ultimate Regret

His Ultimate Love

Upcoming Titles

Chasing Kane

If You know someone with Mental Health issues, Gender Based Violence Victims or you need to talk to someone contact:

Counselling line:0861 322 322

Suicidal Emergency: 0800 567 567

24 hr Helpline:0800 456 789

Ask your friends and Family how they are doing from time to time.

Chronicle Pages Media

Midrand

©Pearl Mampetlana, 2022

©Chronicle Pages, 2022

ISBN: 978-1-998980-04-8

Cover designer: Graphicmart1

Editing: Grammar House

Table of Content

CHAPTER 1

TAY

I have never been so fucking scared in my entire life, it felt like my world was ending right in front of my eyes. My heart pounding like never before, as I run in the heavy rain trying to get to Olivia. Time seems to stand still, then go on, then pause. My soul feels like it's on fire, burning my body in the most painful ways I could ever imagine. She can't leave me, she just can't. Smoke is coming out on the front of the car when I finally reach her and open the driver's seat. Her head is rested on the airbag, and there is no seat belt around her. Blood cascades her forehead.

"Fuck!" I curse and lift her head and push her back against the seat. There is blood between her legs, and I pad her face.

"Love wake up, please." I cry out, but she doesn't wake up or show any movement. I try again and she continues to stay still. I can feel tears running down my cheeks, and I let them flow. I'm not ready to be without her and I'm not willing to.

"Oh my God!" a voice says, and I turn my head to find an old man with an umbrella in his hand.

"What happened here?" he asks, and my mind finally snaps out of it.

"Call...call an ambulance!" I plead with him, and he takes his phone out of his pocket.

"Hang on, I love you so much. If you can hear me, fight..." I push her hair off her face.

A voice asks, "Does she have a pulse?" I place my fingers on her neck and release a sigh of hope when I feel her weak pulse.

"Yeah, but it's weak. Tell them to hurry please!" I request and the man nods. I want to hold her, but I'm scared to move her, scared to make things worse. I feel numb, this is the last thing I expected to happen. I was supposed to take her baby shopping. Out of all people, Donald is the last person I expected to rape a woman. Is that why he chose to represent them for free? To ease his conscious. Olivia was finally moving on and now I'm sure she will go back to square one, and I have no idea what she will do when she gets better. I don't know what's worse? The fact that we finally know the person who ripped her innocence away or the fact there is a video of her trending online that shows what happened. This is utter humiliation and disrespect.

The sound of the ambulance siren brings me back to reality. I move away from the car as the paramedics run to the car with a stretcher bed and the other two guys holding umbrellas.

"It's time for me to go," the old man says looking at me with sympathy. I'm numb and my response is robotic.

"Thank you for your help," I shake his hand, and he nods.

"There is no need to thank me. I did what anyone would have done. I hope she gets better." he says and walks to his truck.

Seeing Olivia wrapped up in a neck brace breaks my heart, and I look away for me not to break down.

"Are you coming with us?" a voice asks.

"I will follow you." I say, and they nod wheeling her to the back of the ambulance. I rush to my car and hop in the driver's seat. I don't bother buckling in and speed behind the ambulance.

I dial Nate's number, and he answers on the first ring.

"Get everyone to the hospital. I mean everyone!" I order and hang up before he can question me.

I pull into the hospital lot and hop out. They wheel Olivia inside, and I spot James and another doctor I have never seen running after her in the direction they took Future weeks back.

I plop down on the chair and throw my head into my hands. I finally let all the tears out. I have never thought I will have to go through something like this, this is the worst thing anyone could go through, and I will never wish it on my enemy. We were so happy yesterday.

"What happened?" a voice asks, and I lift my head to find Nora rushing to me.

"What happened to my baby?" she cries, and Joe pulls her into a hug.

"I don't understand. How..." she sobs, and I close my eyes to stop the tears that are threatening to spill.

I get pulled into a hug and the tears spill more. I feel another hug on my back, and this is a time I'm thankful to have two brothers.

"She will be okay," Nate says and I nod.

They break the hug and look at me, sympathy fills their eyes.

"What happened? Where was she going?" Joe asks and I don't know what to tell him. He doesn't even know Olivia was raped, how am I going to explain how now his daughter is all over the internet? To make matters worse my cousin is the one who raped her. He will hate me, us. His daughter's life got ruined by one of us. How do I explain where she was going when I didn't even know myself? Was she running away from me because Donald is my cousin or did she leave to be alone?

I have no idea if Nora knows or not, but I can't just ask her here.

"I..." I get cut off by a phone ringing, and I let out a breath I didn't know I was holding. Joe takes his phone out of his pocket and answers.

"Yes?"

"I'm sorry but I can't make it there. My daughter is in a hospital and in a very critical condition. Can't you tell me what it is?" he asks.

"I'm afraid I can't, doc," he says, and I wonder what doctor he is talking to. Is he sick? I can't help but wonder.

"Yes, I'm sure. Tell me." he massages his temple clearly stressed and what came out of his mouth shocked the hell out of us.

"What do you mean Grace committed suicide!" he stills, and my eyes widen. What the hell am I going to tell Olivia when she wakes up! Today keeps getting worse and before any of us can react Nora drops to the floor.

"Fuck!" we all run to her and Joe scoops her up in his arms. A nurse tells Joe to follow her.

"What is happening?" Nate asks.

I wish I knew little brother.

5

CHAPTER 2

TAY

"What do you think led Grace to kill herself?" Nate asks after a while. Joe hasn't come back since he took Nora to be checked.

"Did you know that Olivia was raped?" he continues to ask, but I don't have the energy to answer his questions right now.

"The woman I love with all my soul is on an operation table fighting for her life Nate! Your questions are the last thing I want to answer right now!" I snap without meaning to.

"I'm sorry." Nate says softly making me feel guilty. I ran my hand over my face in frustration.

"Look, I didn't mean to snap at you like that." I pat his shoulder and walk in the direction Joe went to.

I knock on the white door and enter. Joe is seating on a hospital bed holding Nora's hand.

"How is she doing?" I ask and close the door behind me.

"The nurse said she will be okay. It's just the shock of receiving bad news in less than 24 hours," he says, and I nod.

"Do you know the full story on what happened? I mean Grace?" I ask and take a seat opposite him. I may have not liked Grace, but she was Olivia's mother even though she didn't deserve the title. If it wasn't for her getting pregnant then I wouldn't have had Olivia. She was a bitch, and I didn't like how she treated her own daughter, but she was still her mother and there is nothing I can do to change that.

"I called the doctor that was treating her, and she said Grace swallowed a bunch of pills she was being treated with. She didn't take the medication like they thought she was. She saved up and when they were enough, she swallowed all of them." Joe explains.

"So, she has been planning her own death without them knowing?"

That's sick.

"Pretty much," he says, and Nora's head turns side by side indicating that she is waking up. She groans and lifts her hand to her head.

"Hey?" Joe says softly.

"God! My head hurts" she says opening her eyes.

"You hit your head hard," Joe tells her.

"Do you remember what happened?" I ask. She turns her head to look at me then back at Joe.

"You said something about my sister committing suicide which is ridiculous. Grace is a lot of things but not a quitter," she says and my heart breaks making me feel week. If she is acting like this then how will Olivia take it?

"It's true Nora. Grace committed suicide." Joe says softly and Nora shakes her head repeatedly in denial.

"No, no, no, no. You are lying to me. Grace would never do something like that," tears fall down her cheeks. Joe goes to her, and pulls her into a hug, and I push my chair back and walk out giving them some privacy.

"Any update?" I ask my brothers and they shake their heads. I slide down the wall and sit on the floor with my knees-up and my hands in my hair.

An hour later, Joe and Nora walk to us.

"Hey, I'm sorry about Grace?" I say to Nora, and she nods.

"Any news about Olivia?" she asks, and I shake my head no. A door opens and I turn to find two guys pushing a hospital bed and we rush to her.

"How is she?" I ask the nurse.

"The doctor will be with you in a sec," he says. James and a woman walk out and I rush towards them.

"How is she?" Nora asks and James takes off his gloves.

"She lost a lot of blood and since she wasn't wearing a seat belt her body took some large impact that caused her to lose the baby." James looks at me. I think I kind of knew that she will lose the baby.

"What baby?" Joe asks and I curse under my breath for forgetting to tell him.

"Your daughter was 7 weeks pregnant, and she was well aware of it sir," James tells Joe.

"She will be fine right?" Nate asks this time.

"Yes, we sedated her for the next 24 hours for her body to heal a little. She will have to wear a neck brace for two weeks as you saw a while ago. She fractured her right arm. Make sure she attends all her check-ups and I think a little therapy will speed up the process." James explains, and we all sigh in relief.

"Thank you so much!" Joe shakes James' hand.

"Just doing my job sir."

"I will keep you updated if anything changes. Now if you will excuse me, I have other patients to attend to." With that him and the woman walk in another direction.

"Okay, can someone please tell me what the hell happened?" Joe demands, his eyes on me.

"I... God! I don't know where to start." I push my hair out of my face.

"Start from the beginning."

"I think it's better if you read it yourself." I say and Nate takes out his phone.

"What do you mean read about it?" Nora asks. Nate hands his phone to Joe and Nora. I wait impatiently as he reads, noticing his knuckles turning white due to his grip on the phone.

"What the hell is this crap about Olivia getting raped by your cousin?" he yells. Nora has her eyes closed and I can only assume she knew about Olivia's past.

"It's true Joe," I say softly.

"When did this happen and where the fuck where you?" he asks, his breath on my face.

"It happened four years ago, Joe. I didn't know that it was Donald or knew until Olivia told me about it." I explain.

"Bullshit! You knew and still protected your shit of a cousin!" Nora tugs his hand, but he easily yanks it away. I have never seen him so angry.

"Joe, please. He didn't know." Nora says and Joe turns to her with fire in his eyes."

"You knew?"

"Yes, I knew but I didn't know it was Donald too." She informs and Joe let out a disbelief laugh.

"Wow! Apparently, I don't know shit about my daughter and the people around me are just a bunch of liars!" he says, and Nora tries to calm him down.

"It's not like that, Joe." I try to explain.

"Get out!" he shouts pointing to the exit.

"Excuse me?"

"I said get out! You and your brothers. I don't want to see you any of you close to my daughter."

"Joe!"

"Not now Nora!" he pushes her away.

"She is my wife. You can't just tell me to stay away from her." I state. I don't know how long I can hold on to this bullshit. I know he is hurting but we all are.

"Well, she is my daughter and I'm telling you to stay the fuck away from her!"

"I'm not going anyway until Olivia herself tells me to stay away from her." I snap and feel a hand on my shoulder.

"I don't fucking care! She is my daughter and I make decisions for her right now."

"Where the fuck were you when she was raped you asshole!"

"Let's take a walk," Nate says, and before I can tell him to fuck off him and Andrew tug me away from Joe.

CHAPTER 3

TAY

"What the fuck was that?" I shrug out Nate's grip. Joe might be Olivia's father, but he has no right to tell me to stay away from my own wife.

"Calm down," Andrew says and I glare at him. How can they expect me to calm down when I'm being forbidden to see my own wife?

"Don't tell me to calm down!" I snap. I'm tired of people telling me what to do.

"We are not the enemies here Tay. We are just trying to help." Nate says gently pulling a plastic chair on the hallway of the hospital.

I sigh and sit down, "I know." I run my hand over my hair. I look outside, and it's already dark and still raining. The paparazzi are still outside, and I fucking want to kill them. They don't know what personal space means.

"Do you think she will end things between us?" I ask my brothers the question that I've been avoiding in the back of my mind.

"Why would she end things? You are not guilty." Nate state.

"She can't blame you for something you had nothing to do with or had any control over." this time Andrew says.

"But Donald is my cousin and when she sees me, she will see him. All of us." I let out my fears.

"That's ridiculous and you know it."

"Is it though?" I ask Nate. Even he doesn't have an answer to my question.

"Olivia loves you and I'm sure you guys will get through this too. You might not know the love you have for each other, but we do. We have seen it with our own eyes. Day in and day out of arguments, lies, and betrayals, love but you always choose each other. If that isn't love, then I don't know what it is because I have never seen anything like what you guys share." Andrew says confidently and Nate nods in agreement.

"We have been through so much that I don't think love is enough to keep us together, not anymore." my heart breaks at the bitter truth that reality has hit me with. No matter how hard I try to convince myself that everything will be okay, I know deep down that, things will never be okay again. Maybe it's better if I stay away from her as Joe requested. Give her a chance to heal, to think about what she wants without me clouding her judgment.

"I think It's better if I stay away from her for a little while, "I tell my brothers, and they look at me like I have lost my mind.

"Why the fuck would you do that?" Nate asks.

"I don't think I can face her after witnessing what Donald did to her." I state. The video is imprinted in my mind playing repeatedly. Olivia painful sobs as she lays still in her own pool of blood unable to move. Donald's moans, grunts, and groans as he takes pleasure from her pain.

"Tay, Olivia needs you. She needs you to be strong for both of you." Andrew says.

"Olivia needs people who won't remind her of Donald around her. Us being close to her will make her hate us." It will dig an even bigger hole in my heart. I honestly don't know what to do anymore. A part of me wants to stay here with Olivia, but another part of me keeps telling to go away. That when Olivia wakes up, she will not want me anymore and I will instantly become blind without her.

"Don't do it." Andrew pleas as I stand up. I ignore him and walk back in the direction where Joe and Nora are at.

"Tay!" a voice yells after me causing Joe and Nora to look up.

"I need a favour from you?" I tell Joe. He stands up with Nora by his side.

"You are no condition to ask me for a favour after what your cousin did to my daughter," he glares at me.

"Joe!" Nora says softly and he sighs in defeat.

"What is it?"

"I need you to take care of her for me please?" I request and he scoffs.

"I will take care of her more than you have had, trust me. She has shed enough tears in your hands and that family of yours. I will make sure she doesn't this time and if I could turn back the hands of time, I wouldn't have forced her to get married to you either or anyone for the matter of fact." he says harshly and in some way he is right. Olivia had shared many tears because of me. Maybe this would be for the best, for her, for us.

"Joe you can't just make a choice for her. Let her wake up first then, she can tell us if she wants Tay out of her life or not." Nora argues.

"Nora it's okay. I understand him." I say and give Nora a hug.

I walk away from the woman who has my heart and my soul with her.

"You are making a big mistake," Nate says as we step out of the hospital.

How is Olivia doing Tay?

Did you know all this time?

I ignore the questions and we rush to our cars.

"Maybe, maybe not," I say and hop in the driver's seat. Nate gets into the passenger seat with Andrew in the backseat and we drive the car into the traffic.

I don't know if my decision was wrong or not, but right now it feels like it is the right thing to do. God! I love her so much, but I can't be selfish. Whether I like it or not Donald is my cousin and in Olivia's eyes, he will always be the guy who had ripped her innocence away from her. I can only hope this is not the end of us, the end of our story. Sometimes I feel like the universe is conspiring against us. Something always pops up to separate us. How much can our hearts stay together and not break into unfixable pieces?

Not so long ago we were planning our family, and now it's all gone. I stop at the red light and lightning strikes. A storm starting just like the storm inside me. A storm I don't know how to handle. The light turns green, and I pass the intersection.

Ten minutes later I park in front of the house. Nate and Andrew run to the house leaving me behind. I punch the steering wheel taking all my anger on it. I rest my forehead against it and soon tears fall down my cheeks.

Why us, why us, why us, why us, why us, why us, why us, why us, why us, why us, why us. These words keep repeating in my head. I feel like I'm losing my mind, maybe I've lost my mind. I throw my head back against the car seat and shut my eyes. Wishing all of this could be a dream, a nightmare I will soon wake up from when I open my eyes. I start the car and drive back to the empty road driving in circles. I find myself in front of Jessica's house. I need a distraction from losing my mind, I need to stay sane. Jessica could help, I need to work. Work will help drown my thoughts and take me away from this emotional turmoil.

I climb out of the car and into the hard pouring rain. I take my time walking to the front door mainly because I love how the rain is pouring down on me, washing away my sins. I knock on the door and wait for Jess to open.

"Oh my GOD!" Jess says when she sees me.

"What are you doing here and why did you get yourself soaked. God! Come in." she pulls me inside and closes the door.

"There is a room next to mine that you can use to clean up." she informs, and I nod. I climb the stairs and walk to the room she told me to use.

I strip out of my clothes and get in the shower. I lazily stand under the shower. Ten minutes later I step out and dry myself.

"Hey?" Jess says softly.

"Did you manage to take the video down?" I ask as I pour myself a glass of whiskey.

"Yes, but the damage is already done," she says, and I nod in response and gulp down the whiskey.

"Do you remember when I told you I wanted to buy a hotel in Cape Town?" she nods.

"I want you to get all the information you can gather about the current owner." I request and she nods again.

"How is she?" I take the bottle and a glass to the couch.

"Better." I give a short answer.

"Why are you here Tay and not with your wife?" she asks with curious eyes.

"I'm here because I decided to stay away from Olivia until she tells me otherwise. I am here because I can't go inside my own fucking house because her scent is there. I am here because I'm afraid to sleep alone without her by my side and I'm here because I need someone to talk to other than my brothers. Is that too much to ask for?" I snap without meaning to. I have a death grip on the glass.

"Tay?" Jess says softly, and I shake my head no.

"Don't. Please." I place the glass on the coffee table and pour another drink.

"I..."

"Just go to bed. We will talk tomorrow." she hesitates but nods. She walks out of the living room and pads the stairs. I grab my glass and walk to the small fireplace. I stand next to it looking at the fire like it is the most fascinating thing in the world.

"I love you so much Olivia. You don't how much I want to be beside you right now." I whisper into space and gulp down my drink.

CHAPTER 4

TAY

A hand shakes me, and I groan opening my eyes. Jess has a mug in her hand, and I sit up on the couch. I massage my temples to get rid of the headache.

"I made coffee" Jess says and places a black mug on the coffee table.

"Thanks." I wrap my hands around the mug and bring it to my lips.

"I know it's none of my business, but I think you should slow down with the drinking for a little while, Tay." I stop midway and look at her.

"You are right, it's none of your business!" I snap and place the mug on the table. No longer in the mood for coffee.

"Think about your health, you know what..."

"You don't know a damn thing about my condition." sleeping here was a mistake. A big mistake.

"I may not know anything about it, but I know mixing booze with your condition is deadly. You could die, Tay!" she is now screaming at me which a bit surprising. Jess has never raised her voice at me, not even once.

"I feel like I am dead anyway. What is the point of living?" I say out loud and Jess gasp.

"Don't say such, you hear me? Life is a journey with a lot of potholes on the road, but you must be strong enough to get yourself and the car to the other side rather than feeling sorry for yourself. It won't get you anyway, and you know it. You are one of the strongest people I have ever known. You never give up no matter what. Every problem has a solution, remember?" she turns my words against me. I don't know what to do or feel right now.

I remember when I first saw Jess, she was so lost and all alone. Just a little girl afraid in the world all alone when Mom brought her home with us. She almost ran into her with her car because she came out of nowhere. It was a miracle that the car stopped at a foot away. I remember her fearing all of us, thinking we will hurt her. She was a victim, she witnessed something she shouldn't have. She witnessed her parents getting brutally murdered, something no 15-year-old should witness. The reason she became a PI and worked with the police. Mom paid for her studies and when she graduated her mission begun. She hunted all of them down, every single one of them and now they are in jail.

I blink as a soft hand touches mine. "I know right now it seems like everything is coming to an end, but it's not. There's always a silver lining at the end."

Tears threaten to spill at the corner of her eyes.

"Do it for Olivia. You love her, right?" she says and continues,

"Don't drink yourself to your own death please." she pleads. I don't intentionally drink because I want to kill myself, I drink because somehow, somewhere it helps me stay sane and balanced. Dealing with the virus was never easy for me, the medication that came with it. At some point, I wished I was normal, with a normal lifestyle without endless medication. Nate has never had a problem with it. He wakes up every day like it's normal, takes his medication on time then go on. I have never heard him complain to mother about it. I pull my hand away and lean back against the soft material.

"I really don't want to talk about this," I say, and she nods in understanding.

"What is happening with Donald and David?" I ask.

"They are standing trial next week Friday if you want to go. Olivia might be asked to tell the side of her story,"

"Olivia is not ready to do that yet. Talk to the person handling the case and tell them that Olivia can't stand trial. I'm sure Donald's story and the evidence will be fine." she nods, and I check the time on the wristwatch. 9 am, it reads.

"I have to go," I say and grab my car keys.

"Keep me posted if anything new pops up," I say, and she nods holding the door. I walk outside and quickly bring my hand to my face to shield my eyes against the bright sunlight.

"Fuck! it's like it never rained last night," I say under my breath and walk around to my car. I hop in the driver's seat and reverse the car out of the house driveway.

My mind wanders off to Olivia and if she is okay. Is she better than she was yesterday? Has she woken up yet, did she ask about me? Is she mad at me or afraid. I sigh at the thoughts occupying my mind and speed down the road.

Minutes later I park my car in front of my house and hop out and place my car keys inside my pocket whilst opening the door. The TV is on the news channel and this time they are reporting about Olivia's accident. I walk to the kitchen to find Nate, Rachel, Andrew, and Future looking depressed.

"What's with the faces?" I ask and sit on the barstool next to Rachel. They all look at me as if am crazy.

"How is Olivia?" Rachel asks and I sigh.

"If you want to know so bad about how she is doing why don't you go to the hospital?" I snap at her and receive a deadly glare from Nate.

"I'm sorry. I didn't mean for it to come out so harshly." I apologize, and she nods with a smile on her face.

"Why are you still here?" I ask looking at Andrew and Future.

"What do you mean by 'why are we still here?' "Andrew asks confused.

"Your new house remember? Why aren't you there? Don't tell me that you are not moving in anymore because of what happened? Because that would be ridiculous."

"We can't move out when things are like this, Tay" Future says, and I shake my head.

"I guess I have to kick you out then."

"What do you mean by that?" Andrew asks.

"I want you both out of my house before the end of the day, am I clear?"

"No," Andrew says being stubborn.

"It wasn't a request; it was an order." with that I push the stool back and get on my feet. I pad the stairs to my…our room. The bed is unmade, and everything is pretty much the way I last saw it.

Expect she is not here.

I take a shower and dress in sweatpants with a long-sleeve t-shirt folding the sleeves of the shirt up until my elbow and I make the bed.

After making the bed I dial James' number and place the phone on my ear waiting for him to answer.

"James speaking?"

"How is Olivia?" I ask.

"Who is this?"

"You know that already now, how is she?"

"Tay, I know..." I cut him off getting irritated.

"Look I know about your feelings for Olivia which you shouldn't be having considering she is married. But now..."

"I don't have feelings for Olivia," he says quickly with a bit of panic in his voice.

"I hate liars you know. Just keep your hands and your mouth to yourself and we will be fine. Now back to what I called you for, how is she?" I walk to the bay window.

"She woke up half an hour ago." my breath hitches in my throat.

CHAPTER 5

OLIVIA

My body hurts, all over. I try to move but Nora holds me down.

"Easy there. You just woke up honey, don't overdo it." she says softly. The accident is still fresh in my mind. My car driving into a tree. I thought that was my last breath. I know for a fact I lost my baby, and I don't how I feel about that.

I shut my eyes and the video plays in my mind over, over, and over again. My breath hitches in my throat, and I pull my lower lip between my teeth to keep myself from crying. I wonder how many people have seen it. How will I ever show my face again to the public? Everyone will be pointing fingers at me, and I don't think I can survive that.

I hear footsteps approaching the bed and I open my eyes to find James and dad in front of me.

"How are you feeling?" Dad asks, and I look around for Tay and his brothers. As if Dad can read my mind he says, "He is not here. Neither are his brothers, and he is not coming back." he informs. I don't know how I would have reacted if he was here. Donald is his cousin. His cousin destroyed my life, and I don't think I can just ignore it and get back with him. Because of his cousin, I had to take sleeping pills to be able to sleep and I might start to take them again because when I close my eyes all I see is that video.

Because of him, I lost a lot of things, my confidence and intimacy. How can I go back to Tay when his cousin ripped my innocence away from me? He made me barren. I lost way too much, and I don't think I can play a happy family when his family destroyed my life.

"But if you want to see him, I can tell him to come see you?" Nora's voice has hope in it.

"N…No. I don't want to see him." I don't even recognize my own voice. I know for a fact that I still love him so much, and it scares me. I think I'm out of my mind for still loving him after everything.

"Good" Dad says with a smile on his face.

"Um, if you guys don't mind, I would like to talk to Olivia in private?" James says for the first time since he got here.

"Okay." Nora grabs her, and she walks out with dad behind.

"How are you feeling?" James asks and seat on my bed.

"Like I have been hit by a truck." I joke but James doesn't laugh.

"Olivia this is serious!"

"I know." I sigh and turn my head to the side to look at him. All I want is to forget. And that it wasn't Tay's cousin who raped me, and Tay would be by my side right now. I wish I could live with Tay in the world I designed in my mind for us. No problems and no family drama.

"Did you know?" I ask. If he knew that it was Donald and didn't tell me then I don't know what I will do.

"Knew what?" he asks confused.

"That...that it was Donald who did It? "I ask not sure if I want to know the answer.

"No. I didn't." he continues,

"You said you didn't want to report it, so I didn't look at the rape kit results because I knew I wouldn't have been able to keep quiet if I knew." he places his hand on top of mine, and I don't move my hand. Somehow his hand provides the comfort I have been seeking since I woke up.

"I took it to the police," he says softly, and I nod.

I really hope that they don't ask me to come and testify because I don't think I will be able to do it. I am not ready to face him yet or the world. I am pretty sure my face is all over the front pages of all newspapers and magazines. If only I could change the past I would. I wouldn't have gone to that party but I would have stayed in my dorm room and read a book.

James breaks me from my drowning thoughts, "I have to tell you something."

"I know I lost the baby." I stare in space and my mind wonders what would have been like to have a family with Tay. Will we ever have a family together? The odds are against us.

"I'm sorry."

"When will I be able to go home?" I change the subject. I don't want to talk about the baby. Some part of my mind thinks it's better things turned out this way. I wouldn't have been able to tell Tay the truth anyway.

"Tomorrow. You don't need to be here. I will give you some painkillers for the pain." I nod and release a deep breath I didn't know I was holding. I hate hospital and no matter how hard I keep trying to stay far away from them something pulls me back in.

"Can you also give me some sleeping pills? I think I will have trouble sleeping." I say, and he looks at me for a moment then nods.

"Get some rest." he pats my hand and walks out.

'Get some rest', his words keep playing in my mind like a mantra. If only he knew the things I see when I close my eyes, then he wouldn't ask me to get some rest. Will I ever get over what happened to me? Will the nightmares ever stop?

The door opens and Nora enters.

"I'm so happy that you are okay now," she says with a smile that doesn't reach her eyes.

"Me too. Are you okay?" I ask not sure if what I'm seeing on her face is right or not.

"Y... yes I'm fine." she sits on the plastic chair next to my bed and holds my hand.

"Why are you doing this?" she asks.

"Doing what?"

"Distancing yourself from Tay. He is still your husband you know?" I yank my hand away.

"You know why. How can you expect me to be with him after I found out it was his cousin who raped and assaulted me?" I yell without even realizing it.

"That's right, his cousin, it wasn't him who did that to you. You can't blame Tay for his cousin's doing. Tay can only be held accountable for his own mistakes." she defends him, and I stare at her in shock.

"Whose side are you on?" I'm yelling now but I don't care.

"I'm on your side Olivia "I scoff and shake my head.

"Doesn't seem like it to me," I mumble.

"Why don't you talk to him? You can't just leave things like this. "She suggests.

"I'm not ready."

"When will you be ready?" I wish I knew the answer to the question too.

"You guys belong together. Everyone can see that too." she says, and I don't if that's true or not.

"I guess if it's meant to be then it will be." I respond.

I can only hope on that sentence. I don't mean to be so cruel to him, but my heart has been hurt so many times I lost count. Mostly by him. One can only forgive so many times. Sometimes I wish I didn't love him so much then it would be easier to move on. He is like damn heroin, I'm addicted to him in ways a person shouldn't be addicted to heroin.

CHAPTER 6

OLIVIA

"There is something I have to tell you," Nora says avoiding my face.

"What is it?" I ask.

"It has to do with your mother." she grabs my hand, and I don't know what to think of it. I can't handle any more bad news; my heart won't be able to handle it.

"She...she co..." the door opens revealing dad. He walks in holding two cups of coffee.

"I got you coffee," he tells Nora and hands her the cup.

"What were you going to tell me?" I remind Nora and her eyes widen in surprise.

"Um...Nothing. It's nothing." she places her cup to her lips and takes a sip.

"Okay?"

I feel like she is hiding something from me, both of them. I don't know who to trust anymore. Everyone around me is either lying or keeping something from me. I'm tired of it. I wish I could pack and leave without looking back or worrying about someone. I wish someone could just take me away from this bitter love.

Why does love hurts so much? Why does it have to hurt to love someone? All I ever wanted was someone to love and for them to love me back. It's like I'm paralyzed from all this love, it keeps hitting me ten times harder than the last time and I don't know if I have the energy to keep on fighting. I'm emotionally and physically drained.

I wonder if Donald ever regretted what he did to me. Did he enjoy destroying my life? I wish I had the guts to face him and ask him why? Why he did that to me? Why did he continue even when I begged him not to?

Dad breaks me from my consuming thoughts by asking, "You are moving in with us, right?"

"Yes, but I have to go to Tay's place to pack my clothes first," I inform dad.

"I can go get them for you?" Nora suggests.

"No, this is something I have to do myself." Nora nods and I release a breath I didn't even know I have been holding. I have no idea what I will do when I see Tay. What I know is that I can't be with someone who is related to the person who destroyed my life, my courage, and made me very shallow for almost five years. No matter how much I love Tay, this is something I will not do. I will fight it if I must. He helped me grow as a person, made me confident again, helped me become vulnerable, helped sleep with the lights off, and more importantly, showed me how it feels to love someone with all your heart. I will forever be grateful for that.

"We have to go, but we will come back tomorrow before you get discharged," Dad says breaking me from my drowning thoughts again, and I nod.

"Try to get some sleep, honey." Nora kisses my forehead and I watch as they walk out. I turn my head to the bay window and it's already dark outside. I didn't even notice it was this late. I sigh and close my eyes to sleep with my worst nightmares resurfacing.

The next morning, I wake up to James in the room.

"Hey, how are you feeling today?" he asks.

"Fine," I say and clear my throat.

"What time is it?"

"Half-past ten." He informs.

"When am I getting discharged?"

"If you get ready then I guess you can leave anytime," he says, and I nod in understanding. I hate hospitals with all my heart, and unfortunately for me, I visit it more than any other place.

"Can you help me up please?" I request and he nods holding my shoulders. He helps me walk to the bathroom.

"I will get a nurse to help you." he informs and closes the bathroom door. I sigh and try to use my left hand to undo the hospital gown but end up hurting myself. The bathroom door opens and a nurse walks in.

"Let me help you with that," she says and undo the hospital gown. She helps me dress up in black tracksuits.

"Thank you," I say, and she nods and walks out. I find Nora and Dad waiting for me outside the room talking to James.

"I was just giving your dad instructions about the painkillers and sleeping pills," James says and I just nod. I don't care about anything right now, all that is on my mind to get the hell out of this hospital.

"Well, I guess I will see you at your next appointment?" I nod and Nora hooks her arm with mine to help me walk. It's a little painful when I walk.

We step into the elevator, and I hold on to Nora's arm as the lift goes down. Minutes later, we step out and walk to the exit. Flashes snap in my direction and Nora walks us quickly to the car trying to avoid the questions been thrown at me by the journalists.

Olivia how do you feel about Grace committing suicide?

Was she always depressed?

Are you going back to Tay?

Olivia is it true that you will not be testifying against Donald?

Is it true you knew all along who raped you and decided to keep quiet?

"What did you say about my mother?"

Did the Payne family threaten your family, and is it why you married Tay?

Nora forces me into the car before the paparazzi can answer my question.

"Give me your phone," I demand, she hesitate but a glare makes her hand her phone to me. I google Grace Ferguson and news about her suicide appear.

"We were going to tell you" dad

"Drive to Tay's place please," I inform him and we stay silent for the rest of the drive.

Dad pulls into Tay's driveway and Nora helps me climb out. We both walk to the door and knock.

The door opens revealing Nate.

"Sister-in-law!"

"I just came for my clothes," I inform, he nods and steps aside.

"Nate, who is it?" A voice that makes me weak in the knees asks. Tay comes to halt when he sees me. He has bags under his eyes and his eyes are red from lack of sleep. He opens his mouth to say something but close it again when he doesn't know what to say to me.

"I just came for my clothes." He nods and Nora helps me up the stairs. My heart is a little bit disappointed that he didn't react to seeing me. I have no idea what I was expecting him to do but this far from it. He didn't even say anything to me.

We enter our room, well now it will be his room only.

"The suitcase is in the closet," I inform Nora and she walks to the closet. I sit on the bed, trying to get the familiar comforting scent on me one last time. Seconds later, Nora walks out with a black suitcase and some of my clothes in her hand.

She places the bag on the bed and fills my bag. We spend half an hour packing.

"This is it," Nora says and zip up the bag.

"Ready?" she asks, and I pull my lower lip between my teeth to calm my breathing.

"Can you please give me a moment?" she nods and walk out.

"Is this the end of us?" a new voice asks and my breath hitches in my throat. Tay stands in front of me, and I look up to his eyes. He looks broken and vulnerable. It's taking every fibre in me not to hug him and tell him that everything between us will work out.

"You know this can't work anymore?" I say softly hoping he will understand.

"Why? Why can't it work? I don't see the reason why we can't work?" his voice crackling. Tears are threatening to come out and I can see he is holding back.

"You know why Tay. It just can't be." my own voice betrays me.

"You don't even know what you are saying, Olivia. I thought I could stay away, but I can't. I can't fucking stay away from you because I love you. I love you so much it's hard to breathe when you're far away from me. Please don't do this to me? don't end us?" he pleads, and tears fall down my cheeks.

"I can't." I sob and he brings his thumbs to wipe my tears.

"My heart has been hurt so many times Tay. I just can't anymore, I don't want to fight for us this time. I have given you everything, I have nothing to give you anymore." I manage to say through my sobs. I clutch on his shirt to try to stop myself from shaking.

"Don't you love me anymore? You used to tell me that you love me so much, what happened?" his words are a knife in my back. I don't know how he is managing to keep himself from breaking down.

"I never lied to you. I loved you." I place my hand on his face and he places his hand on top of my hand

"Then what's the problem? Why can't we be together?" tears roll down his cheeks and he doesn't bother wiping them off.

"I gave you all of me and I got nothing left. The explosion that happened ruined me to the core. I can't anymore,"

"I love you," he cries and kneels in front of me.

"We are like fire and I'm gasoline. Together we are dangerous."

"That's why we are so damn good together," he reasons.

"At what cost?"

CHAPTER 7

OLIVIA

"We keep hurting and lying to each other! What kind of life is that?"

"Please Olivia?" he begs.

"Stand up?" and he does.

"Tell me you don't love me anymore and I will never bother you again."

"You know I can't do that because I love you. I will always love you." he cups my head and caresses my cheeks with his thumbs.

"Then tell me you don't anymore because if you don't, I will never stop fighting for you, for us." tears prick at the corner of my eyes.

"Please don't make me do it." his eyes are begging me to do it. To take the pain away but I can't because I don't want to tell him I don't love him anymore even if it will get him to leave me alone. A part of me doesn't want him to stop fighting for us, but another big part wants him to give up.

"Then don't end us. It's hard to breathe when you are far away, and I don't want to experience it for the second time. Please I beg you?" he rests his forehead against mine and shut his eyes for a moment.

"I don't want to end us too, but I have to. Every night I close my eyes I see him and feel his hands around me. I just can't do it." I confess.

"You don't have to deal with it alone anymore. We made promises to each other at the altar remember. We promised we will be with each other through thick and thin, and I meant every word. Please don't shut me out?" he pleads. Tears roll down his cheeks and my own join seconds later.

"Tay, I love you, but this is something I can't do. I can't be with someone whose family destroyed my life. You've got to let go of me and move on." I place my hand on top of his to try to let him let go of my face.

"How can you expect me to move on to someone else when all I want is you. I can never love someone else like I love you. I'm yours and will always be yours." my heart melts into a puddle of joy at his words.

"You are branded on my heart. My heart only knows you, wants you, and nobody else. We have survived so many things together and I know we will survive this too. Don't give up on us." he says and brushes his nose against mine.

"You are a good man Tay. I'm grateful for the memories we created together. They are the best thing in my life, and I will always cherish them." I promise. Even though he broke my heart a couple of times, he still gave me the best memories ever.

"Don't you dare? this is not goodbye." his voice cracks and I must use all the energy I have to hold back the tears.

"I'm sorry," I say and before I can untangle myself from him, he moulds our lips together. His lips assault mine and I place my hand on his chest to push him away, but he tightens his hold on me. He keeps assaulting my lips until I give in and kiss him back. He slips in tongue in my mouth, and I moan. His hands go in my hair, and he brings me impossibly closer to him wanting to get as much as he can from this kiss. It might be the last time I get to kiss him, so I respond with the same force. The familiar feeling builds in the pit of the stomach, and I wish I could stay like this forever.

Seconds later he breaks the kiss but keeps his forehead on mine trying to get his breathing back to normal.

"Tell me you didn't feel anything? Tell me you don't ever want to feel my lips on your lips again? Tell me, Olivia." His voice is strong now and I swallow the ball that has managed to form on my throat.

"You don't get to take my heart in full and bring it back to me in pieces. You have no right to do that." I sob.

"I'm not ready to give you up, even if you are ready to give me up. This story is only just getting started. The only way for you to be free of me is if I die." he says and tucks a strand of my hair behind my ear.

"I hope you find someone who will love you as much as I did, I do," I say softly to him and place a small kiss at the corner of his lips and walk to the door leaving Tay sobbing.

I enter the living room to find Nate busy typing on his phone. He looks up and locks his eyes with mine for a few minutes. He stands up and walks to me.

"Are you guys seriously separating?" Nate asks and I nod since I don't trust my voice.

"But why? Why do you let other people destroy what you and Tay have?" he asks and leans against the couch.

"I'm doing what is right. Your family destroyed my life. Donald is your cousin, that will never change. I don't want to end up turning our love into hate. I don't want to hate you guys, so I think it's better if I choose me." I say and Nate looks at me for a moment trying to get my words to sink in.

"I hope you know what you are doing. Tay is not the one who destroyed your life, and I don't think he deserves to pay for someone else's sins. Just saying." he shrugs.

"Thanks for everything you have ever done for me." he nods, and I walk to the front door not looking back once.

I slip into the passenger seat and dad reverses the car out of the driveway, and into the empty road. I watch as Tay's house becomes smaller and smaller until I can't see it anymore.

"Aren't you going to ask anything about your mother?" Nora asks.

CHAPTER 8

TAY

Three days, 3 days have passed without her, and they have been the worst days of my life ever. I thought I could change her mind. Life without her is miserable and I can't sleep properly. I eat just because I must eat, not because I'm hungry. I don't know what to do to convince her that we need each other, that we are each other's breaths. She doesn't answer my calls or maybe she blocked me and not being able to hear her voice is driving me crazy.

A sound breaks me from my painful thoughts, and I look at my laptop to see I have a new e-mail. I have thrown myself into work in attempts to forget her. It only works for a while and then I will go back to thinking about her again. I don't know what to do anymore.

I open the e-mail and it's about one of my latest projects. My phone rings before I can read the e-mail.

"Danny?" I push my hair off my forehead and lean back on the single couch.

"I called to ask if you got the e-mail, sir?" I hear yawns and I look at the time at the bottom corner of the laptop. 2 am, it reads.

"Yes, I did Danny. Get some sleep. We will talk tomorrow." I hang up and stand up from the couch and face the bed. I don't know when last I slept on it. It feels so foreign sleeping on it without her. Most of the time I end up falling asleep on the couch while working.

I stretch my arms and walk to the door. I walk through the hall and notice Nate's door open slightly, and music coming from it. Andrew and Future moved to their new house, and Nate and I are the only ones left. I find him punching a black boxing bag in the middle of the room shirtless, sweat dripping off his body. Black hand wrap gloves on his hands and a song I don't know playing on. I forgot how bad his taste in music is.

"It's bad to stare you know?" he says still punching the bag and I lift myself from the door frame and walk inside.

"What are you doing still up?" I seat on the bed.

"I could ask you the same thing." he fires back, holds the bag, and looks at me.

"I was working." I shrug and he raises his eyebrow at me questionably but doesn't say anything. He takes off his gloves and hands them to me.

"And?" I ask, looking at the gloves.

"You look like you need it more than I do," he says and opens a bottle of water.

I take off my shirt and put the gloves on. I stand in front of the bag and start to punch. The bag turns to Donald, and I find myself punching harder than before not caring about the pain. Everything I have been going through these past 3 days comes back like a waterfall. The breakup and everything I have gone through.

"Woah! Slow down, man." A hand pulls me back and I break out of the trace I have been in. Nate is looking at me with a worried expression.

"Are you okay?" he asks and I shake my head no. I was able to keep it together for the past 3 days and now I'm breaking down like a little girl.

"It hurts. I feel like I can't breathe!" I say trying to calm my breaths.

"I'm sorry man. I can't even begin to imagine what you are going through."

"I wish I could just forget her, her smile, her laugh. Her laugh!" I laugh a little when her smile flashes before my eyes.

"Her laugh is the most beautiful sound I have ever heard. Her small giggles lit up my day." A smile plays at my lips.

"Fight for her. Don't give up." Nate encourages.

"I can't anymore. I must let her go like she did to me. There's no point in fighting for something that is dead anyways." I take a sip from the bottle.

"You and I both know you don't mean anything you just said. You two are stronger than you think."

"I miss her," I say to myself, but I know Nate heard me.

"Then go get her."

"It's not that simple."

"Distance is nothing when one has a motive," he says and gulps down his water.

"Who said that?"

"Who said what?" he asks, confused.

"We both know you didn't come up with that line." A small smile forms on my lips.

"I'm hurt. My own brother!" I raise an eyebrow at him, and he sighs in defeat.

"Fine, Jane Austen said it," he confesses, and I let out a laugh.

"Since when do you read Jane Austen? When did you even start to read novels?"

"You would be amazed at the things I do because of love," he says, and I can't let help but laugh at an image of Nate reading a novel.

"Yeah, we are whipped".

"You have the worst taste in music." I comment.

"We both know that's not true. This song is trending and touch that spot in your heart. Just listen to the lyrics." he restart the song and I listen. He is right, the song has a meaning. A girl dates the guy just to get back at her ex. The guy is hopelessly in love, and he doesn't care that she is using him.

"I can also teach you some moves?" Nate says breaking my concentration on the song.

"I don't dance." I remind him. I hate dancing and everything that has to do with dancing. Maybe it's because I have never been good at it even though I never tried.

"Come on, live a little." he laughs. Nate has been the only one good when it came to trendy stuff.

"Are you going to Grace's funeral?" Nate asks and I walk out of the door.

CHAPTER 9

OLIVIA

I stare at the people before me, I don't even half of the people that came. I still couldn't believe it is her funeral. I can't fathom the fact that she killed herself. I don't understand why she would do something like this. Was the pain too much for her? Didn't she want to live anymore? I wish I could talk to dead people then I would ask her why she did it.

My hand grabs hold of the letter she left for me in my pocket.

"I was given a letter by my father from mom. I didn't have the courage to read before but now I have," I spot the Payne brothers at the back in black suits and sunglasses. They came. My mother's coffin stands in front of me.

I take it out and open it, finally finding the courage to read it.

Olivia,

My beautiful, my one and only daughter. I'm a coward. This is the first time I have written a letter to anyone; it feels so weird writing all I have been feeling and felt on a piece of paper.

My mind forms an image of her laughing with tears rolling down her cheeks while writing this letter.

I didn't have the courage to tell you this in person, so I found courage in a piece of paper. You don't know how happy I was when you forgave me. I know I didn't deserve your forgiveness or your visit. I know I was never the mother you always wanted, and I was never a mother to you and for that, I will forever be sorry. You are an amazing daughter, Olivia. Any mother would love to have a daughter like you. A daughter who is selfless, loving, smart, always forgives those she loves, and who would do anything for her people. Nora raised a gem, and I will be forever grateful to her for raising you when I couldn't even after what I did to her. You will be an amazing mother, my love, I know it. Don't be afraid of motherhood, you will be amazing.

I wipe the tears that managed to roll off my cheeks with the back of my hand. I place the piece of paper to my chest at the thought of the son I never got to have. I wish she was here to tell me all those things she wrote in this piece of paper. I continue to read.

I remember one day I watched you play mom with your dolls Nora got for you. You were beyond happy that day, you had that sparkle in your eyes and I enjoyed watching you. It's my favourite memory of you. You were talking to those dolls as if they were human, which was hilarious and adorable at the same time. You are so beautiful and inestimable, and I'm sorry for forcing you to marry Tay. I was blind and all I cared about was money and my reputation. I had no idea that I was destroying your life by trying to live my life through you. I know you wouldn't understand my doings when you find out why I ended my life, but I couldn't take the pain anymore. Your forgiveness gave me what I needed to finally breathe, to leave. I love you so much even though I never showed you. I don't regret having you. I will always be with you wherever you are.

Your mother,

Grace.

Quiet sobs escape my mouth and I shut my eyes clenching on the paper. I never thought mom's words would affect me so much. I don't how to feel that she had a memory of me. I seriously didn't think I would wake up to find my mother dead. It shocked me to the core.

Nora helps me sit down and the rest of the service goes by quickly.

"Are you sure about your decision?" she asks and tucks my hair behind my ear as we walk to our car. She places a kiss on my forehead, and I sigh relaxing against her soft lips.

"Yes. I need it. This place doesn't feel like home anymore." She breaks the kiss and I put the paper back in my pocket and take a deep breathe.

"Are you going to tell him, I mean Tay?" I pull my lower lip between my teeth trying to come up with a solution. Seeing him here already brought up emotions I have been trying to bury, and I don't trust myself when I'm near him.

"I don't know, I haven't decided," I confess.

"You have to tell him Olivia. You can't just up and leave without telling him. He is still your husband."

"How am I supposed to tell him that I'm leaving tomorrow. Not for a vacation but for good?" I snap without even meaning to. Honestly speaking I don't want to see Tay's face when I tell him that I'm leaving. It will break me more than him.

TAY

I pull into the courthouse driveway and climb out of the car with Nate. I have been on edge since this morning at the funeral and couldn't do anything. I just hope Donald pays for what he did to Olivia.

"This feels so weird," Nate says as we walk towards the double door entrance.

"I know." I agree. I didn't go to my father's hearing, none of us did.

We pass policemen and walk into the courtroom. There are rows for people to seat, and Nate and I sit at the last two rows. There are few people present and Donald is in a suit sitting alone. Eight members of the jury are seated in the front.

"Where is his lawyer?" I ask myself, but don't pay too much attention to it.

"All rise in court," a voice says, and we all stand up. A woman in a black gown enters holding a light-yellow folder. She sits down and the policeman tells us to sit down.

Judge Dlamini, it reads on the small board in front of her.

"This court is now in session. Case 3334." She opens the folder and looks straight at Donald.

"Where is your lawyer?" she asks, and Donald stands up.

"I will represent myself, your honour." He informs.

"As you wish. How do you plead?" She asks.

"Guilty your honour," Donald replies.

"Are you going to tell Olivia about Donald's sentence?" Nate asks as I drive into the empty road. Donald got sentenced to life in prison without the possibility of applying for parole. And we found out David was sentenced to 10 years.

"I don't know. She is not answering my calls." I tell Nate and he stays silent for the rest of the drive to the restaurant since we haven't eaten anything.

Half an hour later, I pull up in front of the small restaurant, and we climb out and walk to the door. We walk to the booth at the back, away from everyone's eyes.

"Hi, what can I get you guys?" a girl asks holding a notepad.

"I will have a cheeseburger with fries and sprite," Nate tells the girl and I look at the menu.

"I will have bunny chow with sprite too," I say when I spot it on the menu, reminding me of the time Olivia took me to the township.

"Okay," the girl says and walks away. I place the menu down and find Nate staring at me like I have grown two heads.

"What?" I ask.

"What happened to township food is gross and unhealthy?"

"And how the hell do you know about bunny chows?" Nate asks still staring at me like I'm crazy.

"Stop staring at me like that. It's creepy." I lean back on my seat.

"Olivia and I once went to a small restaurant she used to go to and made me try it." I shrug.

"Why can't I seem to make you do things, but Olivia can?" he pouts, and I chuckle.

"Because you are not my wife."

"But I'm your bother?" he whines.

"So?"

"That should count!"

"Well, you don't warm up my bed at night." Before he can respond the girl comes back with our orders.

"Can I get you guys anything?" She asks.

"No, thank you," I say, she nods and walks away. I grab the ketchup and pour it on the chips.

"When are you leaving?" I ask and place a fry in my mouth. I will be all alone when he leaves.

"Next week," he answers, and I take a bite of my bunny chow.

"I'm proud of you little bro. I know I don't say it often, but I am." I tell him and he smiles at me.

"Thanks."

An hour later, we pay for our meal and as we walk towards the door, I accidentally bump into someone.

"I'm sorry." I apologize.

"Tay?" a familiar voice says, and I turn to find Ria staring at me.

"Ria!" I say and a small smile plays on her lips. She looks different. I have no idea when the last time I saw her. I never thought in a million years I will see her again. Our breakup was nasty.

"Um, it's nice to see you again," she says and shifts, and I notice a man holding a baby standing next to Ria.

"Um, this is my husband, KB," she informs, and I shake the guy's hand.

"Nice to meet you. Tay Payne." I inform.

"I know," he says with a small blush on his face, and I chuckle. Sometimes I forget I'm not a normal man with a normal life.

"I love what you did with both companies. You are an inspiration; you don't know how long I have been trying to get an appointment to pitch to you. And now you are here in front of my eyes." he rambles, and Ria rubs his back to make him calm down.

"Breath babe," she says and to say it's weird to watch Ria been like that with him is an understatement.

"Why didn't you tell me you knew *Tay Payne* personally?" he emphasizes my name to make his point.

"You never asked, "Ria says and Nate chuckles beside me.

"Does he live under a rock or something? Everyone knows you and Ria used to date." Nate whispers next to me.

"About that?" I turn to Nate.

"I had everything that associated me with Ria removed, maybe that's why he doesn't know," I inform.

"Um, do you have a minute?" KB asks breaking Nate and I's conversation.

"I'm afraid no, but here is my personal number." I take out the small card from my pocket and hand it to him.

"Give me a call next week and I will try to squeeze you in." he nods looking at the card like it is the most fascinating thing in the world.

"See you soon," I say to KB. Nate and I walk out.

"Are you ever going to tell me what happened between you and Ria?" Nate asks as he opens the passenger door.

"Nope," I say popping the 'p'.

"Tay wait?" a voice shouts and I look up to Ria running in my direction.

"Can I talk to you for a minute?" I sigh and nod. Nate climbs in the car.

"Um, I wanted to apologize for trying to ruin your relationship with Olivia. And for lying to you about the pregnancy. It was stupid and I was not in a right state of mind. I didn't mean to hurt you and the blackmail. I guess I was..."

"You are rambling." I comment and she shuts up. She gives me a lazy smile and pulls her lower lip between her teeth in thought.

"I guess what I'm trying to say is that I'm sorry for everything." She says and watches me.

"It's okay. Long forgotten." She releases a deep breath, and her shoulders relax.

"Thank you." I nod.

"See you around." I say and hop into the driver's seat, I join the busy road and drive home.

"Today seems like it's a day of surprises," Nate says when I pull into the driveway and park next to an unfamiliar car. Olivia is seated in front of the door in leggings and an oversized grey hoodie. Nate and I hop out of the car walk towards the door.

Olivia stands up and tucks her hair behind her ear.

"Hi," I say to Olivia, and Nate glares at me but I ignore him.

"Hi."

"I'm going to see Rachel, so..." Nate grabs my car keys from my hand.

"It was nice to see you again sister-in-law," he says and walks away.

"Um, want to come in?" I mentally smack my head for asking such a stupid question. I don't know why my brain can't seem to form a good question.

I unlock the door and enter with Olivia following behind. I place the house keys on the kitchen island and turn to face Olivia, and what happens next shocks me to the core.

She grabs my face and moulds our lips together. I stumble back a little taken by surprise but manage to wrap my arms around her waist and kiss her equality hard.

CHAPTER 10

OLIVIA

As soon as my lips mould with Tay's, a sigh of satisfaction leaves my mouth. It feels like it has been years since I last kissed him. It feels so right and I'm aware that what I'm doing right now is being selfish, but I can't help myself. I need to feel him one last time, just this one last time.

His hands go around my waist, and he hoists me up and places me on the counter. He moves in between my legs and pulls me impossibly closer to him. I break the kiss and trail wet kisses down his jaw. He moans and tightens his hold on me. I have never done something like this to him, he has always been the one to ignites everything. I suck his neck and my name rolls off his tongue, making me wetter than I already am. I tug his t-shirt, pull away from him to lift his shirt over his head, and toss it on the floor. My hands work on their own and they find his face, but he stops me,

"Wait," he says out of breath.

"We need to talk. As much as I would love to fuck you right now, we need to talk." I ignore him and attack his neck. He puts his hands on my shoulders to try to push me away but fails.

"Olivia...fuck!" he groans, and my lips form a smile. Not so long ago, the roles were reversed. I was the one telling him we needed to talk, and he was seducing me into having sex.

I pull his earlobe into my mouth, and he moans out my name. I love the effect I have on him. He finally manages to push me away and take a step back.

"We really need to talk," he says and runs his hand over his hair. I pull my lower lip between my teeth and look at his hard-on.

"We don't. We don't need to talk to be able to tell each other what we want." I jump off the counter and walk towards him.

"We do need to talk to Olivia. You can't just break up with me and come back like nothing happened. Do you have any idea what I have been through?" He asks, with a soft voice and a little bit of anger. I place my hand on his bare chest and trail it down to his pants.

"Olivia?" he warns, and I slip my hand in his pants. He groans and wraps his arm around my torso. I look at him in the eyes while continuing to stroke him. His eyes roll at the back of his eyes in pleasure.

"I don't want to talk right now. All I want is your hands on my body. I missed you so much." I confess and place a kiss on his chest.

"Please," I beg. He looks at me for a moment and takes my hand out of his pants. He hoists me and I wrap my legs around his waist.

He pads the stairs and into our room. He places me on the bed and hovers over me.

"I missed you too, love." He says and I pull him closer to kiss him. I have no idea how I will tell him that am leaving. All I can do right now is show him how much I love him.

"Fuck! You taste better than the last time." He says and kisses my jaw. He tugs my hoodie and I lift my body to make it easier for him. Good thing I just wore a hoodie only.

"I love you," he says boring deep into my eyes.

"I love you too." I place my hand on his face and he shut his eyes in satisfaction.

Yet you are leaving, my subconscious reminds me. But I push her at the back of my head not wanting to feel guilty for doing this.

Tay places small wet kisses on my stomach going up to my breasts. I arche my back and close my eyes as my eyes roll at the back of the head. Sometimes I forget how amazing sex is with Tay. Every time we have sex it's like it's our first time.

He pulls my nipple inside his mouth, and I moan, clenching the sheets. He hums in respond and continues to suck my nipple.

"Oh, fuck!" I say when he slips his hand in my leggings and play with my clit. I bite the back of my hand to keep my moans down.

"Don't do that," before I can ask what? He rips my hand away from my mouth.

"I want to hear every moan you make. I want to hear how much I affect you. I want to hear it all." He declares and pulls off my leggings along with my shoes. He gets between my legs and bends down to my throbbing sex.

"Already dripping." He comments and places his fingers on my sex.

"So ready for me." He rubs my clit and without warming, he slips his finger inside me, and I gasp.

"You good?" he asks, and I nod. He pecks my lips and start to pound in me. I wrap my hands around his neck, and he continues to assault my sex.

"Fuck! You are so tight." He adds another finger and pressure builds at the pit of my stomach. He pulls his fingers out before I can come, and I look at him in disbelief.

"As much I love to see you come, I would rather much you come on my dick, not fingers." He sucks my juices off his fingers and takes off his pants.

He stands bare in front of me, and I gulp at how hard he is.

"Open your legs for me, Love." He orders and I do as I'm told. He gets between my legs, and I try to calm my breathing as he positions himself at my sex. He pushes in but doesn't go all in. He pulls out and this time he goes all in stretching me, and I quickly wrap my arms around his neck. He groans and locks eyes with me. Beads of sweat have formed on his forehead, and he pecks my lips. He starts to move taking me to another blissful world where only he and I exist. Seconds later, he speeds up.

"Oh fuck!" Tay groans and continues to pound into me. Pressure starts to build at the pit of my stomach, and I bite Tay's shoulder without even meaning to.

He pulls out and flips me over so that I'm all on four. I bury my face into the sheets as he slips back into me. My hand clutches on the sheets and he keeps going in and out of me.

He grabs my hair and pulls me back against his chest. One of his arm wraps around my torso and one goes play with my boobs.

"I love you." He speaks. I want to say it back to him, but I can't seem to let the words roll off my tongue. All I can think about is how good it feels to be in his arms again. The only arms I fit in.

He thrusts one last time and we both collapse on the bed breathing hard. He pulls out and lies next to me.

"That was amazing," I say and turn to watch him. He pulls me closer to him.

"I'm glad you came back." I hum in respond and push his hair off his forehead.

"We have so much to talk about." he tucks my hair behind my ear.

"I'm leaving." I blurt out.

"Okay, I will come and see you tomorrow after work." he places a small kiss on my nose.

"No." I sigh.

"Okay? I will call if you don't want me to stop by. I understand that your dad still doesn't like me because of...."

"Tay I'm leaving the province." I say and his fingers stop playing with my hair.

"What do you mean you are leaving the province?" he sits up.

"I'm going to Cape Town and I'm not coming back at all." I confess.

"So, this is what? Goodbye sex?" he yells and get up from the bed.

"I had to say goodbye somehow." I wrap the sheet around my naked body.

"You had to say goodbye? Are you hearing yourself right now Olivia? I can't believe this." He runs his hand over his hair in frustration.

"It's just a two-hour flight, Tay. Why are you so mad?" I yell and throw my hand in the air.

"You are freaking moving Olivia. I have every right to be mad and not to mention you just used me minutes ago." He pulls his pants up his legs.

"You know I could have just left without telling you anything, but I am here. Telling you."

"Is that supposed to make me feel honoured?" he scoffs.

"First you break up with me and now you are freaking leaving?" He takes out a t-shirt from the bedside counter draw.

"It is for the best. We have hurt each other more than we have loved each other, Tay." tears prick at the corner of my eyes. I knew he wouldn't take the news well. I shouldn't have come here, but my heart had to overrule my head.

"That's bullshit and you know it, Olivia." he walks out the room.

CHAPTER 11

OLIVIA

I sigh as the door slams shut behind him and I sit on the bed with the duvet still wrapped around my naked body. I knew he wouldn't take the news well. I don't know what the hell I was thinking coming here. I should have just left without saying anything. I grab my clothes from the floor and dress up. I pull my hair tie from the pocket of my hoodie and pull my hair into a messy ponytail. I place my hand on the doorknob and turn to look at the room I used to call mine one last time.

"This is it." I say, take a deep breath and walk out leaving everything behind.

I enter the kitchen to find Tay standing by the kitchen island and a bottle of water in front of him. His head down in defeat and his hands at the edge of the counter.

"Why? Why are you punishing me for something I didn't do?" he turns his head in my direction.

"I'm not punishing you, Tay. This was bound to happen sooner or later. We are a mess." I say and tuck a strand of my hair behind my ear.

"I'm more of a mess without you. Please don't leave me." he walks to me and take my hands in his.

"I have decided Tay. I already got an apartment and it's paid. I need to get away from this place."

"What about our marriage?" his voice cracks at the end.

"I have already spoken with my lawyer. You should get divorce papers soon."

"But I want you, all the time." He closes the gap between us.

"I want you too, but I need to work on finding myself and I really want to Tay. I was 21 for God's sake when I was thrown into this marriage. I want to do what people my age do, explore, and learn more about myself without having to worry about anything else." I confess. Part of me going is because I can't take it anymore. I'm suffocating.

"If you want to travel the world then I can take you wherever you want, just don't leave me." He runs his hand over his face.

"We can figure this out together, we can also go for marriage counselling. I just need you to stay with me. Please stay with me?" he pleads, but my mind has already been made up.

"I can't. So much has happened here that I would rather forget, and for me to forget I need a change of environment."

"What about the family we were planning to have? Still, want?"

"What family? When I can't even carry the baby full term." I blurt out and quickly place my hand over my mouth, my eyes wide open. Tay's eyes move to mine, confusion written all over his face.

"What do you mean by that?" he asks. I open my mouth to try to explain but close it again when I'm unable to come up with an explanation.

"Don't make me call James, Olivia." he warns.

"I found out that I have abdominal trauma which prevents me to complete the pregnancy to full term, "I confess.

"When did you find out about this?" he asks calmly which scares the shit out of me.

"The day James was constantly calling and leaving messages, "I explain, trying to calm my breathing. I have no idea what's going in his head right now and his face is not giving anything up.

"Where you ever going to tell me?"

"I don't know."

"I seriously don't know who you are anymore Olivia. What happened to your 'no more secrets'? " He quotes my words.

"Maybe you leaving is not such a bad idea anymore. I don't know what to expect with you anymore."

"I didn't mean to keep it from you. I feared how you will take it. I wanted to protect you from the pain." I try to reach for his hand, but he takes a step back. I pull my lower lip between my teeth to keep myself from crying. The last thing I want to do is cry right now, I feel like I have done a lot of crying that I lost count.

"You had no right to make that decision for me, Olivia. It was mine to make, only mine." He shouts, and I don't even flinch since I'm used to his mood swings.

"Would you have still wanted me if you knew though?"

"Of course, damn it!" he throws his hands in the air.

"I love you. Don't you get that already? I love you more than anything in this world. Yes, I want to have a baby with you. But there are many options we can choose from. There are millions of babies out there looking for parents and women who are willing to become surrogates. I would never leave you because of that." he says.

"I don't run like you always do. I'm not you Olivia?" he snaps, and I glare at him.

"What is that supposed to mean?" I'm so tired of this conversation. It keeps going in circles. One minute we are talking about me leaving, then about me withholding information about our baby from him.

"You are running away instead of staying and dealing with our problems, your problems."

"That's not what I'm doing"

"Really? Because from where I stand it looks like you are running. Ever since we found out about Donald, you have never visited him in prison to seek closure or attended his hearing." He points out.

"How do you expect to solve your problems when you keep running?" he raises his eyebrow at me.

"I didn't come here to discuss your cousin. I came here to say goodbye because I'm leaving tomorrow." I walk past him and grab Nora's car keys on the kitchen island.

"Great! I hope you find what you are looking for." He says and shifts so that I can pass.

"Goodbye Tay," I say to him, but he ignores me. I sigh and walk to the door and to Nora's car. It is already dark, and I check the time.

7 pm. It reads as I reverse out of the driveway and into the empty road.

I drive back to my father's house. Half an hour later, I park in front of the house and hop out of the car. As I enter the house I'm greeted by the smell of food.

"Ah! You are just in time. I made oxtail!" Nora beams at me.

"I'm not really hungry but thanks." I place a kiss on her cheek and climb the stairs to my room.

I walk into my room, take a Prep pill, and start packing my bags. By the time I finish packing it's 10 pm. I get into my pyjamas and get under the duvet. Sleep creeps in as soon as my head hits the fluffy pillow.

The next morning, I wake up to my buzzing alarm. I groan and shut it off, placing my hand over my face. Seconds later, I roll off the bed and walk to the bathroom. I brush my teeth, strip out of my clothes after and step into the shower. Half an hour later, I step out of the shower and dry my hair. I walk to my wardrobe and grab the clothes I didn't pack. Black skinny jeans, a black t-shirt, and a black hoodie, and white tennis shoes.

A knock comes from the door as I finish putting my shoes on.

"Come in," I say and Dad walks in.

"I've come to help you with the suitcases." he informs. I have two large suitcases only.

"Okay." I stand up and let him pull my bags out of the room.

Nora is standing next to the door when we come downstairs with a sad look on her face.

"I will give you guys a minute," Dad says and walks out of the house wheeling my bags.

"I can't believe you are leaving!" Nora says and pulls me into a hug.

"I will just be two hours away. You can visit anytime." I reason.

"Are you sure about this?" she asks once I break the hug.

"Yes." I sigh and she gives me a small lazy smile.

"Take care of yourself and call every day, okay?" I nod and hug her one last time.

"Okay, I got to go." I chuckle and rush to the door as I hear a honk.

"I love you!" I shout as I close the door behind me.

I climb in the passenger seat and buckle up. Dad reverses out of the driveway and into the quiet road.

The drive to the airport is silent aside from the playing radio. I look out the window, looking at the city I grew up in one last time. Nerves kick in when I see the airport coming closer and closer to my sight.

O.R. Tambo airport

Dad drives into the airport lot and parks next to the entrance. I sigh, undo my seatbelt, and hop out. I grab one suitcase and wheel it to the entrance.

"You have your ticket?" Dad asks as we wait on the benches, and I nod showing him my ID and ticket. My mind wanders to Tay. Is he here? I can't help but look around hoping to see him.

"Are you expecting someone?" Dad asks when he sees me looking around.

I clear my throat, "No." he looks at me for a moment and nods.

"Flight 176, flight 176 please report to gate 5." a feminine voice says through the speakers.

"Take care of yourself." Dad pulls me into a quick hug and pecks my forehead. I nod and break the hug. I take a deep breath with my bag in both my hands looking at people moving around. Some going to gate 5. I take one last deep breath and take a step forward not looking back.

I take the window seat and look out the small round window. I sigh and buckle up. People pass and a guy with dirty blonde hair seats next to me.

He turns to look at me and says, "Hi."

"Hi," I say back and lean back against the seat. Minutes later, everyone is seated and nerves kick in. I have never flown to any place or left Gauteng. I have also been afraid of the plane even when I have never boarded it. I have seen a lot of movies to stay away from it.

"Ladies and gentlemen, welcome onboard flight 176. We are currently third in line for take-off and are expected to be in the air in approximately ten minutes. We ask that you fasten your seatbelts in the meantime and secure all baggage underneath your seats or in the overhead compartments. Please turn off all electronic devices, phones, and laptops. Smoking is prohibited for the duration of the flight. Enjoy your flight!" a voice says, and I try to breathe as the plane keeps on increasing its speed.

"First time flying?" The guy next to me asks and I nod. My stomach is in knots.

"How old are you?" He asks and takes a bite of his granola bar.

"21." I reply and look back at him wondering why he wants to know about my age.

"And married?" he says looking at the ring on my finger. My fingers go to the ring and play with it to calm my nerves.

"Something like that."

"Don't tell me you are running away from him because if you are, it's stupid to keep his ring. I would sell it if I were you." He suggests.

"I'm not running away"

"Looks like you made it!"

"Huh?" I say confused.

He points to the small window, "We are already in the air." clouds welcome me when I turn to glance. I didn't even feel it when it took off.

"Hi, can I get you guys anything?" A flight attendance asks.

"Two glasses and a bottle of red wine please," the guy tells the girl and she hands them to him.

"That's all for now. Thank you" she nods and moves to other people wheeling the tray.

"You do know it's early for a drink, right?"

"We have to celebrate you surviving your first ever flight," he says, and pops open the wine. He grabs a glass and pours the red liquid inside. He hands me the glass and pours himself too. I sigh and bring the glass to my lips. I take a sip and notice him staring at me.

"Why are you looking at me like that?" I ask.

"Have we ever met somewhere? I feel like I have seen you somewhere, but I don't remember." He says and I swallow the lump in my throat. I silently pray that he doesn't recognize me and anyone for that matter.

"I don't think we have met." he shakes his head as if to clear his head and places his glass on his lips.

"Olivia by the way." I introduce myself leaving my marital last name behind.

"I'm Dick." I choke on my drink, and he chuckles patting my back.

"Yeah, I get that a lot. I also don't know what my parents were thinking naming me Dick." he informs, and I finally get my breathing back to control.

"Sorry," I apologize.

"It's okay." He leans back in his seat and takes his headsets out of his bag. He plugs them on his phone and inserts them in his ears. I look out the window sipping my wine and minutes later a voice starts to sing. I frown and look back to Dick and find him singing. A few people also turn to look at the person who decided to ruin their peace.

Have you ever had that moment when you have your ear sets in and singing along thinking you sound exactly like the singer? Yep, that is what is happening right now. Dick is even taping his foot on the floor singing SMA by

Nasty C which sounds horrible coming from his mouth. I grab his phone from his hands and press pause. He takes off his ear sets from his ears.

"What was that for?"

"That was for my sanity. God! You sound worse than a broken record." I inform and he scowls.

I sleep for the rest of the flight.

"Hey, wake up" a hand shakes me for the fourth time, and I finally open my eyes.

"God! You are so difficult to wake" Dick grabs his bag from the compartment and I stand from the seat.

"I know." I grab my small bag and we both walk out.

"Here is my number if you ever need a tour guide." he doesn't even ask me if I want his number and just put them in my phone.

"It was nice to meet you!" with that he walks away with only his back bag. I sigh in exhaustion thinking of going to the baggage claim. After claiming my bags I wheel them to the exit. Fresh air and noises welcome me. People walking out and some going in. Taxis dropping people off and taking them away. I wheel the bags next to the road and signal a taxi.

A taxi pulls in front of me, and the driver climbs out of the car and walks to me.

"Let me help you with that miss." he grabs my bags and take them to the car boot.

"Thanks," I say and hop in the backseat.

"Where to?" The driver asks as he buckles up. I take out my phone and open the text the landlord texted me with the apartment building address.

"Here," I show him the text and he nod. He pulls into the busy road, and I look out the window.

Half an hour later, he pulls in front of the apartment building. There are a few cars parked in the lot.

"Thank you." I hand him the money and hop out of the car. I open the boot and take out my bags. I watch as he drives away, and walk to the building in front of me. At the lobby I find a woman dressed in a dress suit standing next to the reception table talking to the receptionist.

"Hi, my name is Olivia Ferguson. I spoke to a woman called..."

"Ava Austen," the lady in a dress suit says holding her hand out to me to shake.

"Nice to meet you."

"Same here. Here are your keys." She hands me the apartment keys.

"If you encounter any problems, call me." I nod.

"I hope you enjoy your stay with us, Ms. Ferguson." I nod and she walks away.

CHAPTER 12

TAY

I gulp down the rest of the whiskey. I have lost count of how many drinks I have had since morning. She didn't even hesitate to board the plane. She left and didn't turn back. She left me. I throw the bottle of whiskey against the wall screaming. I flip the mattress and everything that I can get my hands on.

Someone starts shouting my name but all I see is Olivia leaving. She might not have seen me at the airport, but I was there. A part of me was hoping she would turn back and come back to me.

"Tay calm down" a familiar voice yells. Nate touches my shoulder and I drop on my knees to the floor tugging my hair.

"She left." I sob. Nate stays silent. I can sense he doesn't even know what to say to me to make me feel better.

"She didn't even hesitate. She left me. I lost her. It's over." Tears stream down my cheeks, and I don't bother wiping them off.

"I'm sure she will come back man." I chuckle and lean my back against the back of the bed.

"There is no need to lie to me, Nate. Give it to me straight. I can take it." I wipe the tears and Nate leans against the wall across me.

"I thought you guys worked things out yesterday?"

"She seduced me into having sex with her because she was leaving today. It was goodbye sex!" I inform and run my hand over my hair.

"I'm sorry. You more than anyone deserve to be happy." Nate says sincerely.

"I feel like I'm cursed you know?" Nate holds his hand up.

"Hold that thought," he stands up and walks out of the room. I take a moment to look at the mess I've made. The mattress is on the floor along with the duvet. The lamp is also on the floor destroyed and glasses scattered around. Feathers everywhere. The bedroom door opens, and Nate walks in with a bottle of whiskey and two glasses.

He sits next to on the floor and hands me the glass. He pours the liquor into my glass.

"You were saying?" He reminds as he takes a sip from his glass.

"I was saying I feel like I'm cursed" I gulp the drink in one go.

"Why do you think so?" He asks pouring me another drink.

"I finally found the woman whom I love with my entire life, but all this time it felt like I was fighting just to be with her. And now that I think about it, I never got her. There was always something that wanted to separate us." I say and take a sip of my drink.

"Don't say that Tay. She might have left but you are still married to her"

"For how long though? It only a matter of time until she sends me divorce papers." I gulp down the rest of the drink.

"Maybe I don't deserve her. I lied, insulted, and betrayed her yet she stayed by my side."

"It's good to have someone who loves you no matter what, you know. I have fucked up so many times, but she stayed. I really fucked her up in so many ways, all the lies I told. She stayed by my side even after I tried to get her infected with the virus."

"Yeah, she is one hell of a woman. I thought she would file for divorce" Nate adds.

"There were times I felt like I should let her go but my heart wouldn't let me. The thought of another man touching her makes me sick. A part of me always knew she would leave one day. She's young, 21 and I'm 26. She deserves a better man." I grab the bottle of whiskey and bring it to my lips and take a gulp. I throw my head against the bed and hand the bottle back to Nate.

"Age is nothing but a number. You know that." Nate reminds.

"I know, " I agree.

"It's just a part of me has always reminded me that she could do better than me. I have hurt her so much. I have made her cry more than I ever made her laugh since the beginning of our relationship." I pour out my feelings to my little brother. Sometimes it amazes me how good of a listener Nate is.

"It's not too late to make her laugh." he suggests.

"Her moving away means she doesn't want me anymore otherwise she wouldn't have left."

"Then follow her and fix it?"

"You make it sound simple" I grab the bottle of whiskey and take a huge gulp.

"It is simple"

"Come on Tay. You have always said you wanted to expand Payne Corporations. This is the chance to do it." I look at Nate and take another gulp.

He pats my shoulder and walks to the door. I sigh and use the bed as support to stand up. I walk to the bathroom with wobbly legs and strip out of my clothes. I turn the shower to cold water and step in. Half an hour later I step out and wrap a towel around my waist. I walk out of the room to a guest room and throw myself on the bed and close my eyes to deep sleep.

OLIVIA

I throw myself on the bed and look at the ceiling. I have been unpacking my stuff for the last three hours and to say I'm tired is an understatement. My stomach growls in hunger and I roll off the bed and enter the living room to make something to eat. The apartment is small but beautiful. It has one bedroom, a living room, a bathroom, and the kitchen. Everything is white and there is a TV planted on the wall. A single white couch facing the tv and two white chairs next to the couch. A coffee table. A balcony that gives you the view of the beach. I can hear the waves crashing. I light my phone and it's 8 pm.

I step outside at the balcony and dial Nora's number. She answers on the third ring.

"I was beginning to worry," she says, and I chuckle.

"Sorry I didn't call sooner. I was busy unpacking." I inform and hear a sigh.

"How is the apartment?"

"It's good."

"Are you okay?" she asks.

"I will be."

"Get some sleep and call me tomorrow, okay?"

"I will." I promise and hang up.

Silence greets me when I walk back inside. I fill a glass with water and gulp it down. I walk to the bedroom, undress, and get under the duvet without putting pyjamas on, and sleep welcomes me.

I struggle as a hand pulls me to an alley.

"Shut the hell up!" he says and pushes me against the wall. I wince in pain and stare at the dark blue eyes staring back at me like a piece of meat. I try to push him away, but his knee connects with my stomach. I let out a cry of pain bending, but a hand connects with my face.

"Help!" my voice comes out weak and I fall on the concrete floor. A leg connects with my abdomen, and I let out yet another painful cry. Tears roll down my eyes.

"Please stop!" I beg and the guy comes into my view but this time, brown eyes are staring back at me.

"Tay!" His lips form a smirk and my heart pound against my chest.

"Did you really think I care about you?" He lets out an evil laugh grabbing my hair harshly.

"I don't care about you. You were just a puppet in our game, and you fell for my lies." He brings my face close to his. His breath fanning my face.

"You are ugly and needy. Did you really think I would love someone like you? your body is ugly with those scars. It's a miracle that I haven't puked on it yet. Get this through under that stupid head of yours once and for all." He moves to my ear.

"I don't love you and I will never will." He throws me back on the floor and stands up. I lift my head up to find him and Donald staring back at me with evil smirks.

I jolt awake and look around my room. I touch the spot next to me and find it empty. Tears stream down my face, and I pull my legs to my chest and rock back and forth trying to calm down. This dream is worse than the others. I wipe my tears and grab my phone on the bedside counter. I dial Tay's number and place the phone on my ear. It rings and goes to voicemail causing me to cry more. I need to know that the dream wasn't real, it can't be real.

I try again and this time it goes straight to voicemail.

I speak into his voicemail box, "Tay!" I sob into the phone.

"I can't do it. I can't sleep and this time the nightmares are worse. The first one I had of you, you were just watching Donald have his way with me and you didn't do anything to stop him. You just watched!" I cry into the phone and tug my hair crying.

"It felt so real. You were there!" more tears roll down my cheekbones.

"The second time, you didn't just watch. You said that...that you never loved me. You said my body disgusts you!" another sob escapes my mouth, and my phone slips out of my hands and on the bed. I hug my legs and let more tears out.

I run to the bathroom and strip out of my clothes and step into the shower. I turn it on and slide down the glass and to the tile floor. All I can think about is that dream and Tay. I really needed him with me right now. For him to hold me and tell me that the dream wasn't real. To tell me he loves me, and he would never do something like that to me. I pull my legs to my chest as the warm water cascade down my body.

I thought a change of environment will make them go away. I thought I would be able to leave the past behind. I don't want to rely on pills to sleep. I'm tired of them. I want to be able to sleep without being afraid of what kind of nightmare I will have.

I stand up and turn the shower off. I step out and grab a towel and wrap it around my body. I stare at my face on the mirror and the girl staring back at me looks like me, but she is broken. She is a mess. Her eyes are puffy, and her nose is red from all the crying. I scream and punch the mirror multiple times and I don't feel anything. The pain, the voices and anger I feel inside is something I have never felt before. I can't contain it.

I unwrap the towel and drop it on the floor. My hands go to my small scars on my stomach. I trail after them with my finger. I grab a glass in the sink and hold my hand out. Tears fall down my cheeks. I have been drowning and still drowning and I can't keep myself from falling. I have been holding on to the last hope I had in me, but the pain is too much, and I can't bear it anymore. I tried to fight it, but no one can help me. I'm lost. Too lost to come back. I grip the glass and slit my wrist and all I can release is tears, no pain, nothing. I'm far too gone, and no one can help me. The feeling of helplessness and all I want to escape from this life. Be at peace, a life of peace. Is this what mom was feeling when she did it too? I let myself down. I can feel myself fade away as I slit the other wrist and I welcome the peace that comes with it.

"Please forgive me." I slip into darkness.

TAY

I groan and try to find a comfortable position to continue sleeping but I keep tossing and turning. I sigh and open my eyes. I push my hair back and search for my phone. I might as well do some work since I can't sleep. I roll off the bed and tighten the towel around my waist and walk to our room.

"How the hell I'm I going to find my phone in this mess?" I say and sigh. I grab black joggers and a long sleeve t-shirt and put them on. I push my hair back and try to find my phone and laptop. I grab the mattress and spot my phone on the floor along with the laptop. I grab them and walk back to the guest room.

I charge my phone and open my laptop to start working. I answer some emails and after a while, I grab my phone and turn it on. I relax on the chair while I wait for it to turn on. I put the password and notifications pop in. I stare at the phone when I see two missed calls from Olivia and one voice message from her. I tap on the message and place my phone on my ear.

"Tay?" she sobs into the phone, and I sit up straight.

"I can't do it. I can't sleep and this time the nightmares are worse. The first one I had of you, you were there, watching Donald have his way with and you didn't do anything to stop him. You just watched!" she cries. I pause the message as I cannot listen to the pain in her voice.

She dreamt of me hurting her. I would never do anything to hurt her and her dreaming of me doing something so awful breaks my heart. I dial her number and it goes to voicemail. I tug my hair frustrated. I grab the phone again and dial the pilot's number.

"Get the jet ready. We are leaving in thirty minutes." I say into the phone and hang up. It has been so long since I used the private jet. I push the chair back walk out of the room to my room and put on my shoes. I walk downstairs and grab my car keys from the kitchen counter and walk out the front door.

I hope into the driver's seat and reverse the car out of the house's driveway. I dial Jessica's number.

"Hello?" Jess says in a sleepy voice.

"You have two hours to find me Olivia's exact location. I want to know which apartment she is in. The tracker I put on her phone doesn't work anymore." I inform Jess.

"Couldn't it wait until morning?"

"It is morning already!" I comment and park my car close to the plane and hop out.

"You know what I mean."

"Just get me the information, yeah?"

"Fine." she hangs up and I walk up the steps.

"I hope I didn't wake you from your sleep too Hailey?" I ask my pilot.

"Not at all, sir."

"What is the destination this time?" She asks as I sit down on the white leather seat.

"Cape Town." I inform and she nods and disappears.

"Would you like something to drink sir?" The flight attendant asks.

"No, thank you." she nods and leaves. I grab my phone and listen to the rest of Olivia's message.

An hour later my phone rings and I answer.

"Yes?"

"Olivia is at the hospital." Jess informs, and my world crashes.

"What do mean Olivia is at the hospital?"

"She tried to kill herself and one of the neighbours found her."

"Is she okay?" my voice cracks. Why would she do something like this? Am I not important for her not to kill herself?

"Yes. They managed to stop the bleeding. She is at Groote Schuur Hospital."

"Thanks."

The jet lands and I rush to the door and to the SUV waiting for me.

"Groote Schuur Hospital." I tell the driver and search the internet and the news are already trending.

Few minutes later the car stops in front of the hospital, and I rush inside.

"What the fuck are you doing here?" Joe asks standing up.

"Olivia is my wife."

"She filed for divorce,"

"I haven't signed them so fuck off," I have heard it with Joe.

"My daughter is at the hospital because of you again! Leave before I call security."

"You think because you were her father for three months makes you the father of the year? I have been patient with you but not anymore. Olivia is my wife and there is nothing you can fucking do to change that, and I think you have forgotten who you are fucking talking to, Joe." He swallows a lump that has formed in his throat.

"No!" Olivia's voice crying has us on alert and we rush inside the room.

"My baby is crying. I need to feed him," she struggles against the nurses.

"Let me fucking go!" she yells, and I make my way to her.

"Hey, look at me? It's okay." I hold her.

"I can't," Joe says rushing outside and I scoff.

"The baby is crying! He needs me. Let go of me! Please," she sobs, her struggles slowing down I hold her tight, and a nurse gives her sedative.

I lift her in bridal style and put her on the hospital bed and follow the doctor.

"What happened?"

"Has she ever lost a baby before?" the doc asks.

"Yes, a couple of weeks ago."

"Did she go to counselling?"

"No,"

"In my view she is suffering from the trauma of losing the baby and amongst many other problems. It's not good to keep things bottled up because when you explode there is no grantee that you survive."

"I understand. I will get on it as soon as possible." I sigh and lean against the wall.

CHAPTER 13

OLIVIA

Tay is standing in front of me with a worried face. I stare at him not being able to form a sentence. I look around and notice I'm at a hospital and there is a bandage around my wrists. He steps closer and pulls me to his chest. He hugs me tight like if he lets go, I will vanish. I hug him with the same thought. Last night memories played in my mind and a sob comes out. I don't know if things will go back to normal or we will break up forever. I sigh breathing in his scent that clams me down all the time. It feels good being in his arms, it feels like home after going away for a while.

He nuzzles his head in the crook of my neck and it feels like I haven't been in his arms in a long time.

"Tay?" I slowly whisper hoping he will let me go because he is crashing me.

"Please let me hold you a little longer. I want to make sure you are real. This feels like a fucking dream. I have never thought I will be able to hold you again after what you did." He confesses and I let him hold because I feel the same way as he does.

Moving to Cape Town was a way to separate me from Tay. It was easier if I did it when I was far away from him, and we would move on with our lives. In my mind, it was that easy but truly speaking I was trying to convince myself more. Tay finally breaks the hug, but his arms are still around me.

I bite my lip as my eyes meet with his. I don't know what to do or say to him.

"Look at me?" He orders. His voice dominating the small room. My eyes meet his again and he stares at me with no emotions on his face, but his eyes are telling a different story.

"Many emotions went through me when I listened to your message. The most shocking part was when you said I hurt you in your dream," He tucks my hair behind my ear and continues.

"I am not my cousin. I many have Payne blood running through my veins, but I am not cruel. I respect you way too much to lay a hand on you. The thought of you getting hurt just makes so mad and want to kill someone." He buries his head in the crook of my neck to control his anger. I stay silent as he slowly breathes in my scent to calm down.

"I would never hurt you, love. At least not physically. You know that, right?" He asks, desperate for me to believe him.

"Yes. I believe you" I tell him, and he sighs in relief.

"You are beautiful with your scars. Don't be ashamed of them. They prove how strong you are my love, and you shouldn't think of yourself so low, okay?" Tay strongly says and I nod.

"You have a beautiful body and I plan on proving to you how much I fucking love it," he declares and my cheeks flush.

"Don't ever try to hurt yourself again? I mean it."

We were supposed to separate forever when I did what I did last night.

"What are you thinking?" Tay asks watching me.

"I still feel like I shouldn't be with you because of...you know," I say truthfully. Tay sighs and wraps his arms around me.

"We love each other, Olivia. No matter how much you try to fight it you know you can't win. I know we can't ignore the fact that Donald is my cousin, but we can try every day to make us work. He is paying for his crimes now."

"Why do I feel like I am betraying myself?" I ask Tay.

"It's natural to feel that way but I am not Donald. Please don't end us because of him. We have been through so much together." Tay tucks my hair behind my ear.

"I'm afraid that I'll end up hating you, Tay. I don't want to hate you."

"Tell you what?"

"How about we take it one step at a time?" Tay suggests and I nod in agreement.

He pecks my lips and stands up.

"When am I getting discharged?"

"Tomorrow. For now, rest.

The next morning, I walk up to Tay sleeping on the couch. The door opens and the doctor walks in and he wakes up.

"How are you feeling today?"

"Better,"

"I'm pleased to hear that,"

"I just need you to sign this and then you are good to go." Tay signs and helps change my clothes.

When we get to my apartment Tay makes some calls and I make my way to the kitchen to drink water.

"Yes, for tomorrow." He says into the phone as he pulls me with him to the couch.

"Thank you." He hangs up and turns his attention to me.

"How are you feeling?" He asks as his thumb draws circles on my thigh.

"Better, I promise." I reply.

"I'm glad you feel better." he says and lock his eyes with mine.

"I missed you," he says and moulds our lips together. My hands go around his neck, and he groans. He slips his tongue in my mouth and I tug the roots of his hair. He lifts me up and I wrap my legs around his waist.

Few minutes later, my back hits a soft material. Tay hovers over me and breaks the hug.

"You don't know how hard I want to bury myself inside you right now. I want to taste every corner of your body. I want to show you how much your body drives me insane but not today." He confesses and a shiver runs down my spine.

CHAPTER 14

OLIVIA

"What? Why?"

"Because you are still recovering,"

"That's bullshit!"

He laughs.

"Please? I need to feel loved?" I beg.

He moulds our lips together and I wrap my hands around his neck. He slips his tongue in and I groan. My hands travel down, and I tug on his t-shirt. He breaks the kiss and pulls his t-shirt over his head in one swift motion and crash our lips together again. My hands move up and down his chest. He breaks the kiss, and trails wet kisses down my jaw to my neck. I throw my head back to give him more access.

He breaks the kiss and pulls away from me.

"What happened?" I ask, confused.

"This needs to go," he says, and before I can ask him what he lifts me up so that I am sitting and pull my shirt up. I lift my hands up and he pulls the shirt over my head and tosses it on the floor.

"Better," he says. I lie back on the bed half-naked. He hovers above me and looks into my eyes.

"You are beautiful, Olivia." His thumb runs over my jaw.

"You have a beautiful body and I'm fucking proud that you are my wife." He pecks my lips, and my heart warms up at his words.

"Don't ever think I will be disgusted with you or your body because of your scars, okay? I love all of you." His eyes show emotion, but I can't make it out since I am not good at reading people. He moulds our lips together and this time the kiss is slow, full of emotion and passionate like the first time we slept together.

I tug the roots of his hair and he groans in my mouth. He trails wet kisses down my jaw, and I dip my head further into the fluffy pillow. He moves up to my earlobe and my hands clutch on the sheets as my eyes roll at the back of my head in pleasure. He pulls my earlobe in his mouth and stars apparel before my closed eyes. It's like am reliving the day we slept together for the first time.

He moves down and pulls my nipple in his mouth whilst playing with the other. I bring my hand to my mouth as pleasure builds at the pit of my stomach. He moves to the other nipple and sucks and bites sending me over to a place I didn't even know existed. He trails kisses down my stomach to my belly button. His hands tug my shorts, and he tugs them down along with my panties. He places kisses on my leg moving up to my throbbing core. He licks my clit and my back arches while my toes dig into the sheets.

"Fuck!" I bite the inside of my palm. Tay lifts his head to look at me with a satisfied smile on his face.

"Don't come." he orders, and I nod my head repeatedly. He ducks his head down again and licks my clit sending me to the edge again. He replaces his tongue with his thumb and moves his tongue to my heat. He licks my folds and I throw my head deep into the pillow biting the inside of my palm hard.

"Tay? I can't hold it anymore!" I inform and he withdraws immediately leaving me a panting mess.

"I told you cannot come yet. I want you to come around my cock." He says and pulls his jeans down. He hovers over me and inserts himself between my legs.

"Spread your legs for me, love?" I open my legs wider, and he positions the head of his length at my heat. He locks eyes with me as he moves his member up and down my heat, teasing me.

"Tay," I moan and that's all he needed to push in. I gasp at how big he feels. It's like he gets bigger and bigger every day.

He groans and buries his head in the crook of my neck.

"Fuck! You feel so good," he says against my skin. I lift his head up and make him look at me.

"I love you," I tell him and peck his lips.

"I love you more," he says and starts to move. He pounds into me slowly and passionately while still locking eyes with mine. Beads of sweat have formed on his forehead.

I wrap my legs around his waist when his pounds increases, and he places sloppy kisses on my lips, eyes, and cheeks.

"You are so tight" he informs and my walls clench around his member, warning me.

"I'm coming!" I say and within seconds we both reach our climax. He collapses on top of me while being careful not to crush me with his weight. We stay like this for about ten minutes.

Tay pulls out of me and throws himself beside me pulling the sheets over our naked bodies. He pulls me against his bare chest and wrap his hands over my torso. He places a kiss on my bare shoulder.

"We have to go shopping. There is no food here in here." He informs and I hum in response too tired to reply.

"And I also need clothes. I can't wear the same clothes until I leave." I hum in response drawing small circles on his hand avoiding commenting on him leaving. He moves my hair to the side and place a kiss at the back of my neck.

"Olivia?"

"Yes?"

"I booked an appointment with a marriage counsellor for tomorrow at nine in the morning." He informs and my thumb stops drawing circles on his hand.

"Please say something?" His voice begs. I honestly don't know what to think or say.

"I really don't know what to say, I'm not really the kind of person to open up about what I'm feeling to other people," I say and continue to draw circles on his hand.

"I know, love. Which is why I booked us this appointment, I want us to be able to communicate better about our feelings and for you to talk about everything that happened to you." He turns me around so that I am facing him.

"I am here to listen to you whenever you want to talk. I will always be here for you, but some things need a professional. I can take some of the pain away, but I can't take all of it away. You need to face your fears like visiting Donald in jail to get closure. The nightmares need to go away forever and not a little while. I don't want you to depend on me or the pills to have a good sleep. I need you to be able to sleep peacefully without me being near you. I want you to live a healthy life. I want us both to have a healthy life together with our children." He finishes his speech and tucks my hair behind my ear.

"I love you," I tell him meaning every word. Words cannot express how much I love him. He is the best thing that's ever happened to me. He has my soul and without him, life is nothing.

"I know love. Sleep, you are tired. We will go grocery shopping when you wake up." he places a long kiss on my forehead, and I bury my face in the crook of his neck breathing his scent as sleep creeps in.

CHAPTER 15

OLIVIA

The fresh breeze makes my hair shield my face and I bring my hand to my face and tuck my hair behind my ear. My elbow is out the window. I watch as the other cars speed along with Tay's rental grey Audi A4. I turn my head to look at him at the same time he turns to look at me. He stares at me for a while and looks back at the road, his elbow sticking out of the window. One hand on the steering wheel. We are headed to the grocery store.

Tay woke me up with kisses all over my face. We took a shower together. I was surprised we were able to get out of the shower, to be honest. It was very tempting to have sex in the shower.

Seconds later, I feel a hand-on mine and I turn and Tay brings my hand to his mouth and he plants a quick kiss on my knuckles. My heart warms up at his sweet gesture. I just hope it stays like this forever. We deserve it after the many struggles we've been through. I hope everything falls into place from now on.

Tay pulls up in front of the mall and we both climb out. People are holding shopping bags and some grocery bags.

"Which one should we start with? Clothes or groceries?" Tay asks as we walk to the entrance of the mall.

"Clothes," I say, and he holds my arm.

"When are you leaving?" I ask. Tay turns to look at me and we step on the escalator going up.

"Tomorrow afternoon. I can only come here on weekends since they need me at the office." He informs and my mood changes. I really thought he was going to stay longer. How will we work on us if he is so far away?

"But that's until I open a branch here in CT," I turn to look at Tay and find him already looking at me. We step off the escalator and turn left.

"Really?" I ask, excited.

He laughs, "Yes, that's what I will be busy with and when I get time, I will come see you," he says, and we enter Edgars.

We walk to the women's section.

"I don't need any clothes," I tell him, but he continues to drag me.

"You need them for the beach. We will spend the rest of the day there before I leave." He informs and grabs a red, high leg out cut, knotted one-piece swimsuit.

"Go try this." he doesn't wait for me to comment on the swimsuit and pushes me into the direction of the fitting room. I roll my eyes and open the fitting room curtains and step in. I place the swimsuit on the small bench and close the curtains. I take off my clothes and put the swimsuit on. The necklace Tay gave me rests between my breasts. My hand goes to the 'T', and I play with it while looking at my reflection. I have never worn a swimsuit before because of the small scars on my belly. I didn't want people staring at me and thinking about wearing this tomorrow makes me nervous.

The curtains open and Tay walks in and closes the curtains behind. I pull my lower lip between my teeth as I watch him watch me in the mirror. He stands behind me and places his hands on my hips and I release a small moan.

"You look..." He lifts his head to look at me in the mirror and bring his mouth close to my ear.

"Like you are ready to get fucked here right now on the small bench and against the mirror." he whispers in my ear, and I close the space between us.

"Imagine watching yourself get fucked. Imagine me behind you and my arms around and pounding into you like my last breath. The thrill of fucking in a store full of people," he pulls my earlobe into his mouth, and I moan. The idea of watching Tay and I having sex thrills me, but I don't know if I should be more scared or happy.

He grabs my hand and places it between my breasts.

"Trail your hand down slowly," he instructs.

"Imagine as if it is me doing that." He says into my ear and my mind takes control and imagines Tay trailing his hand down my naked body.

"Relax your body," he says and his breath fans my neck.

"Now, slip your hand in." He says and my hand goes inside the swimsuit panties and to my clit. I release a moan and rock my back against Tay's already hard member. He grips my waist to still me and a whimper comes out of my mouth.

"Circle your clit," he says seductively into my ear, and I imagine his hand rubbing my clit.

"Yes, like that." he encourages, and my pace quickens.

My back arches and I reach my climax and throw my back against Tay's chest. My eyes to find Tay's in the mirror. I smile back at him, and he kisses the back of my neck.

"How was it?" He asks grabbing the hand I used to pleasure myself and bring it to his mouth. I watch as he licks my folds off my fingers, and I pull my lower lip between my teeth.

"Go...good."

He kisses my neck and takes a step back.

"You will find me outside," with that he walks out, and I run my hand through my hair. My eyes catch my reflection, and my cheeks turn red thinking of what just happened. I can't believe I just did that in a fitting room. I shake my head and take off the swimsuit. I dress back up in my jeans and white pullover. I walk out to find Tay sitting on a couch typing on his phone with two more red swimsuits, a red sundress, shorts, and a couple of his jeans and t-shirts. I love this sight of him. He looks carefree like he is not some big shot businessman in just jeans and a t-shirt with messy hair.

He looks up and places his phone in his jeans. He stands up and grabs the clothes from the couch. I help him and we walk to the cash register. Tay pays for the clothes.

"Let me take these to the car" he grabs the shopping bags and walks off. I walk to the grocery store, grab a cart close to the entrance and walk in.

I grab a pack of cheese, yogurt, and random stuff. I have never been good at grocery shopping. The first thing I think about entering a shop is Doritos.

A cart hits mine, "I am so sorr…"

"Olivia!" Dick says and I half-smile at him.

"It's good to see you again," he says showing me his perfect white teeth.

Before I can respond a familiar voice says behind me sending a chill down my spine, "Hey, babe." A hand goes around my shoulder, and I angle my head to look at Tay and find him staring at Dick with the most hateful glare I have ever seen.

"I'm Tay. Olivia's husband" a smile plays at my lips at how serious his face is. Kevin meets my eyes and half-smiles at me.

"The territorial type, I see. Don't worry I'm not planning to make a move on your wife. I already..." A voice cuts him off.

"I don't give a shit."

Dick laughs.

"Damn girl! If I had a man like that..." He again points to Tay checking him out.

"I would lock him in my room forever. He should illegal!" he whistles.

"I'm still here you know," I say friskily glaring at him.

"Hush, you know I only have eyes for you." He laughs when Tay glares at him and adds, "Chill. I'm gay."

"Call me, okay?" Dick says and I nod. We watch as he pushes his cart to the cash register.

"Well, that was interesting," Tay comments and pushes the cart.

"Where did you meet him?" He grabs bread and put it in the cart.

"We were seat buddies in the flight." I inform and watch as he fills the cart.

"So… Trisha said she can see us at nine in the morning. Are you okay with that?" Tay asks.

"Yes."

"Would you like to have alone sessions with her? "

"Yes."

I play with my fingers on my lap and my leg is tapping on the floor with Tay by my side. I don't know why I am so nervous. I turn to look at Tay and he gives me an encouraging smile and grabs my hand.

"Relax. I promise it will be fine." He says and the door opens revealing a woman holding a pink journal and a pen. She is dressed in a blue dress and black heels.

I feel like my heart is going to pop out of my chest. Last night, I didn't think much about it. Tay and I spent most of the time at the mall and he cooked when we got home. I wasn't nervous as I am right now.

A thumb drawing circles on my hand brings me back to reality.

"Hi, you must be Olivia. It's nice to finally meet you." She stretches her hand in my direction. Tay gives me an encouraging smile. I take a deep breath and grab her hand.

"You too, " I give her a smile.

"My name is Trisha," I nod, and she relaxes on her single white chair. Tay and I are opposite to her on a long black couch facing the big bay window. I think we are on the 4th floor. I didn't really pay attention when we were coming up. All I could think about was how the session will be.

"So, I think I'm correct if I say you guys came here to improve your communication, marriage and to help you be able to solve your problems without hurting each other, right?" Trisha asks us and opens her book.

"Yes," Tay responds.

"Let's start with why guys got married?" Trisha suggests looking at us.

"It was an arranged marriage. I agreed to marry Olivia because of my mother. She was dying and wanted to see me married before she died so I agreed just to make her happy." Tay confesses still drawing circles on my hand and I'm grateful because it calms me down. Trisha nods and writes down something in her book.

"What is your version?" Trisha asks, looking at me this time.

I take one more deep breath, "I was forced to marry Tay." I turn to look at Tay to see his reaction, but he is good at hiding his emotions I can't read him.

"I didn't have a say. It was something I had to do." I say and Tay continues to draw circles on my hand.

"How did that make you feel?" Trisha asks.

"I was angry. I felt like killing my mother. I had different murderous thoughts." I confess and Trish nods and jots down in her journal.

"And what do you guys feel now?" She asks.

"I am glad that her mother forced her to marry me as much as that sounds awful, but I wouldn't have found her if her mother didn't force her. She is perfect and is everything to me. I can't see myself with anyone else in this life. She is beautiful the way she is, and she doesn't even have to try. She is my lifeline, my end." Tay says and my heart pounds against my chest so fast I feel like it's going to pop out of my trunk.

"Olivia?" I can feel Tay's eyes on me waiting for my response.

"I feel grateful every day to have him in my life. He saved me from a dark place, and I love him more and more every day. I don't know what I would do without him." I say and Tay brings my hand to his mouth and plants a light kiss on the back of my hand.

"What dark place is that?" Trisha asks.

This is what I was afraid of. I have been trying to avoid talking about it for a while and I kind of hoped that today's sessions won't involve it.

"You can do it," Tay encourages and continues to draw circles on my hand.

"I was raped when I was in high school. After that I never felt comfortable anytime I was close to men, and I started fearing the dark because he raped me in a dark alley. Every time I turn off the lights, I feel like there is someone close by waiting to catch me off guard and do something to me."

"Go on." Trisha encourages.

"He left scars on my body, my abdomen. They make me feel foreign in my own body. I used to feel mortified of my own body and always made sure to wear tops that would cover them." My voice cracks at the end and I bring my hand up to wipe the tears that managed to roll down my cheekbones.

"Would you like to stop?" Trisha asks and Tay runs his hand up and down my back.

"No." I shake my head no and Trisha hands me a tissue.

"Tay helped me face my fears. He helped me overcome my fear of sleeping in the dark and to love my body the way it is. He made me feel comfortable." Trisha nods and I continue.

"I never knew the guy until recently. I never reported him because I didn't want to be judged and I was scared. Scared of my mother and how she would treat me." I fold the tissue and hold it.

"Then I met James. He helped me. He is the one who found me all bloody and unable to move." Tay tenses a little beside me but continues to draw small circles on my hand.

"He took me to the hospital he worked at. He used the back door because I told him I didn't want any attention on me, and he did as I requested. He also tried to convince me to go to the police, but I still refused. I allowed him to take a rape kit test but never saw the results. He checked on me for a few weeks and from then I changed my number. Less contact with people who knew what happened to me the lesser the pain. That's what was going on in my mind at that time. I wanted to forget it ever happened." More tears stream down my cheeks.

"Bu...b... but the nightmares were real. I couldn't sleep for more than 2 hours and one day I decided to get sleeping pills." I tuck my hair behind my ear.

"I was so tired of the nightmares and lack of sleep that I didn't check how many pills I took, and when I woke up, I was in the hospital."

CHAPTER 16

OLIVIA

"You tried to kill yourself!" Tay turns me around. He looks angry and I pull my lower lip between my teeth nervous. I have always been afraid to tell him. I didn't mean to take so many pills. I just wanted to sleep at the time and when I woke up, I was in the hospital. My parents made sure it never became public knowledge. Only the teachers and my family knew.

"I think you guys need to talk so, we are going to end here today," Trisha says and closes her journal.

"Next session we will continue this talk." We stand up and shake hands.

"Thank you," Tay says and we walk out. He holds my hand as the lift goes down. The elevator beeps open and we step out and walk to the front glass door.

We walk through the lot and his silence is killing me and I don't know what he is thinking. He opens the passenger door for me, and I hop in-and he closes the door, walks around the car and opens the driver's seat and climbs in.

I buckle up and he reverses and drives into the busy road.

"Say something please?" I break the silence after a while. Tay turns to look at me and focuses back on the road.

"What do you want me to say?" He asks.

"Anything. Yell at me. Just say something please," I plead. Tay gets off the lane and pulls over at the side of the road. He stays quiet for a few minutes and unbuckles his seatbelt.

"You tried to kill yourself twice now, Olivia. Why would you do something like that huh?" He turns to look at me. I unbuckle my seatbelt and lift myself from my seat to sit on his lap. His hands go to my butt, and I wrap my hands around his neck.

"I didn't do it on purpose I promise. I was sleepy and I didn't check how many pills I took out of the bottle. I promise I would never try to kill myself no matter how bad the situation is." I promise.

"Why didn't you tell me?" He asks and I run my hands through his hair.

"I didn't want you to overreact on the situation," I say avoiding his eyes. I can feel his eyes on me, and I distract myself by playing with his hair.

"Everything that involves you is important to me. You are my wife. I have all the time in the world if you want to tell me something. You have all of my attention if you want someone to talk." He pulls me closer to him.

"I'm sorry for not telling you," I apologize.

"Anything else I need to know?" He asks and I shake my head no.

"I can't think of anything right now." I kiss his forehead.

"I love you." I whisper but I know he heard me.

"I love you more," Tay places a light kiss on my neck.

"Back to your seat," he smacks my butt and I laugh getting back to my seat. I buckle up and Tay roars the car to life and slowly drives the car back to the road.

"What will we be doing today at the beach?" I ask as the familiar street to the apartment greets us.

"That's for me to know and for you to find out." He says and pulls into the apartment lot.

"Pretty please," I beg as I climb out of the car.

"Nope," he says popping the 'p' and rests his arms around my neck and walk us to the building.

We step into the elevator with two schoolgirls eyeing Tay. He plays with my hand as whispers and giggles fill the small elevator.

The lift stops on my floor and opens. "Ladies." He says, and they giggle while we step out.

"Seriously!" I shrug his arm off me and unlock the door.

"What! I didn't do anything," he lifts his hands up and places the keys on the counter.

'Ladies' I mimic him.

"Is that jealousy I smell!" he smells my hair.

"I am not jealous," I say trying to get out of his hold.

"You are jealous!"

"Whatever!" I step away from him, but he grabs my elbow and turns me around. He wraps his hands around my waist.

"You know I only have eyes for you, baby," he kisses my nose.

"I have a great day of relaxation planned for us so why don't you go and grab that small bag I packed last night." He suggests and my mood lightens.

"You are so cute when you are jealous." He yells when I step in our room.

I laugh as grab the small bag hr parked for us and place it on the bed. I strip out of my clothes and put the one-piece swimsuit on. I dress up in the red sundress on top, slippers, and sun hat. I grab the bag and walk out.

Tay is busy on my laptop.

"I thought we were going to the beach?" I whine. He looks up and shuts down the laptop.

"We are. I was just checking my emails. You know Danny is not reliable." He pecks my lips and grabs the bag from me. He opens the door and I walk out

He grabs my hand as we walk out, and I place the paper hat on my head in attempts to avoiding the scorching sun.

The beach is a five minute walk and when we arrive people are busy swimming, kids playing around. I have never been to the beach, and this is kind of awesome and I'm glad that I'm experiencing it with Tay.

I stop to lay a blanket on the soft sand, but Tay stops me.

"What?" He shakes his head and takes my hand and leads me into another direction.

"Where are we going?" I ask when I realize this side is quiet.

"It's a surprise."

"You know I don't like surprises, especially yours," I remind him of the last time he said he had a surprise for me, and he laughs. There are boats around and a middle-aged man comes to us.

"Hi Tbose," Tay shakes the guy's hand.

"It's good to see you again, man. Where is Nate and Andrew?" Tbose asks.

"Nate is somewhere here in Cape Town, and Andrew is back in Sandton. He has a kid now." Tay informs.

"Wow! Tell them I said hi."

"Oh my! Is this the wife you were talking about?"

Tay laughs, "Yes Tbose. This is my beautiful wife, Olivia," my insides flip at Tay's words.

"You are so beautiful. It's nice to finally meet you."

"Nice to meet you too!" I respond, shyly smiling at him.

"The yacht is ready for you. It was really nice to see you again." Tbose pats Tay on the shoulder and walks past us.

"What yacht?" I ask looking around with my heart pounding so hard I feel like I will drop dead on the ground.

"There." he points in front of us, and I place my hand on my forehead to see a small, black yacht on the deck, not far from us.

"Oh my God! Tay. Thank you, thank you. No one has ever taken me on a yacht before!" I drop the bag on the ground and jump on him. I wrap my legs around his waist and my hands around his neck. He laughs and wraps his arms around my body.

"You are welcome love." he chuckles and puts me down. I don't waste time running to the yacht. It is so beautiful.

There is a bedroom, kitchen, and living room.

"You are seafaring?" I ask when Tay gets behind the wheel shirtless and in just white shorts and black flip flops.

"Yep," he says popping the 'p'

"Don't you think a professional should do it?" I ask, worried. I was so excited that I forgot the yacht will have to move.

"Relax, I know how to work this baby." he laughs.

"I really don't want us to be the next Jack and Rose from Titanic," I comment, and he laughs.

"You watch too many movies." the yacht starts to move, and I watch him with excitement and scared at the same time.

"Why didn't you tell me you had a yacht?" I ask pouring red wine into a glass.

"The conversation about my properties never popped up and I kind of forgot about it since I hardly ever use it. Nate is the one who usually uses it for parties." He says and I nod walking behind him.

I run my hand on his back and he turns to look at me for a second and turn back.

"Thank you for doing this for me," I say, and the yacht suddenly comes to a halt.

"You are welcome," Tay says turning around to look at me.

"You deserve the world, and I will give you just that." He grabs the glass away from me and gulps the drink down.

"Want to go for a swim?" He suggests, and I nod.

"You can go up and I will bring the sunscreens." he says and I walk up the small stairs. The sunlight greets me, and I pull my dress up over my head and lay it on the surface. Tay comes to me with the bag he parked last night. He sits behind me, and I grab the sunscreens lotion to squeeze it on my palm.

"This is peaceful," Tay comments, and I nod applying the lotion on my legs.

"Yeah, it is."

He applies the lotion on my back slipping his hands into my bikini bra.

"Tay!" I moan out when he pinches my nipples.

"Yes!" He says innocently.

"It is your turn... for the lotion," I manage to say.

"I am a big boy. I will be fine." I slap his thigh and he laughs and kisses the base of my neck. He pulls his hand from my breast and stands up.

I grab his hand and stand up too. We walk to the small steps that lead to the back of the boat. I sit on the edge as I watch Tay dive into the water. He resurfaces and pushes his hair back and the sun shines on his face highlighting his handsome features.

"Come in the water," this reminds me of the time in the pool.

"Make me," I challenge. I want to know what he'll come up with this time.

"Is that a challenge, love? Because you will lose." He swims in my direction.

"Not this time," I smirk at him.

"I guess we will have to see then." He says and dives his hands in the water and his white shorts pop up in the water.

"What the..." My words get his stuck in my throat when I see Tay rubbing his length in the water.

"Imagine if you were in the water right now. The things we could do. I could do to you. Don't you want to know how it feels to be fucked in the water?" He moans and I clench my legs together at the thought, my sex throbbing at the thought of him inside me.

Traitor!

CHAPTER 17

OLIVIA

"Are you really going to let me pleasure myself!" I pull my lower lip between my teeth to keep a smile from breaking. I look around feeling as if someone is watching us, but I'm met with nothing but water. I stand up and look at Tay who has a smirk on his face. I dive into the water and resurface just a foot away from him. I push my hair back and open my eyes to find Tay watching me with a smile on his face. Paddling towards him I wrap my legs around his waist and my hands around his neck. His hand goes to my butt, and I can feel his length getting excited.

"I love this," Tay says against my lips. I look into his brown eyes and all I can see is the love he has for me. My heart is pounding hard against my chest. I feel like a lot has changed and happened between us in the last 24 hours. I love this peace we have but I'm afraid to be happy. You know what they say, 'it is the calm before the storm', I don't want to think about it, but my mind has a mind of its own.

"What are you thinking about?" Tay asks, noticing my worried expression.

"I'm afraid to be happy," I admit.

"Why?"

"I feel like whenever something good happens to us, something bad is bound to happen," I tell him.

"There is nothing that can tear us apart now. I promise." he promises and feel his hand sliding my bikini panties to the side.

"Oh!"

"You thought I forgot?" He asks rubbing my clit. I tighten my grip around his neck and waist.

Seconds later, he enters me, and I bite his shoulder at how full he feels inside me.

"You, okay?" He asks.

"It just feels weird, a little bit,"

"You can move," I say after a while, and he swims us back until my back hits the back of the yacht and he tightens his grip on my waist and pounds into me.

"Fuck! You are so tight!" He says pounding into me as I moan out. I tug the roots of his hair and he groans. It doesn't feel the same as when we are doing it on the bed.

"Tay," I moan.

"Yes, love?" He pulls my lobe into his mouth and my eyes roll at the back of my head in pleasure.

"Fuck!" I cuss. He rubs my clit while assaulting my sex. I sink my teeth back to his shoulder at the pressure building in the pit of my stomach.

"Say my name?" He groans into my ear.

"Tay," I say, and he increases his pounds I feel like I'm about to pass out. Our skin colliding and moans fill the ambience of the ocean, I lift my head from his shoulder and rest my forehead against his. He looks dead into my eyes. It is such an intimate moment. Our noses are touching, and our lips are just an inch away from each other, our breaths have become one and he brings his thumb to my lower lip.

"I am so fucking madly in love you, Mrs. Payne." he says and continues.

"You are mine. It will always be you and me." He says and we both reach our climax. We keep staring at each other trying to get our breathing back to normal.

Could we finally have our happily ever after? I don't know but this feels like it.

"I'm going back with you to Gauteng," I say, and Tay's eyes widen.

"Why? Not that I don't want you to come with me but why the sudden change?" He asks and tucks my hair behind my ear.

"I want to visit Donald. I just want to close that chapter of my life so I can move on. I don't want to always go backward every time my past pops up. I want to move on, and I can only do that by seeing Donald, one last time." I say and Tay smiles at me.

"I am so proud of you!" he pecks my lips and slips out of me but still holds my waist.

"But I still want you to stay here if you don't mind?"

"I don't care where we are love, as long as you are with me. We can make a home out of nothing." He says and I run my hands through his hair.

"I have an architect who can design our house here in Cape Town. It will be far from the city, private. Just the way you like it." He informs.

"We can meet him when we get to Sandton," I say and peck his lips.

"Thank you," I tell him.

"For?"

"For everything. I don't know what I would do without you. You are my hero." I tell him and he looks at me for a moment.

"It is quite the opposite love. You are my hero. I was a man with no purpose when you came into my life. I wake up every morning because you are the air of my life. You are my purpose in this shitty life the universe has thrown at us. " He lifts me up and places me on the yacht surface and he remains in the water.

"You know, I never thought once that my life would depend on someone else. I always thought it was ridiculous that people in novels, movies, and telenovelas would die for the woman they love and would do anything for them but now I understood. Being in love is the best feeling in this world and I wouldn't trade it for anything else. I love you Olivia Kat Ferguson Payne." He says and I pull him towards me, and we mould our lips together.

He breaks the kiss, "We better get going. It's getting late." Tay says, and I look the sun that is fading away. He grabs his white shorts floating in the water.

Tay drives us back and when we get back to the apartment it is six in the evening. Tay changes into jeans and a shirt. I pack a small bag for a few days.

"Got everything you need?" Tay asks, I nod looking at the small apartment I call home.

"Good. The jet is ready for us," he says casually as if it is not a big deal to own a jet.

"You have a jet?" I ask as he locks the door.

"Yeah," he says, and he steps into the elevator with a middle-aged woman and a girl about my age.

"Are you not the girl that everyone has been talking about? The one on the video getting raped?" The girl asks, her voice sympathetic and the woman slaps her arm.

"Harsh child," the woman scolds.

"I am so sorry my child. My daughter had forgotten her manners.

"No, it's fine. It is me." I confirm.

"Oh!" She says and gets back to her phone. Probably texting her friends about seeing me. I hate the attention of the media on me. They are wolves waiting to skin you alive. I don't think I will ever get used to it. I tried to keep my life private as much as I could from them.

The elevator beeps open and we step out with Tay holding my bag.

"I think it's time we addressed this situation. We have been quiet and I'm starting to get really annoyed about the rumours they are making about you, me and Donald." Tay says and places the suitcase in the boot of the car.

"Let's do it after I visit Donald," I say and hop in the passenger seat.

"I knew I had to do it at some point. I was just avoiding the inevitable," I say as Tay drives into the less busy road.

"Are you sure you can handle it?" Tay glance at me for a second and turns back on the road.

"I know you don't like people knowing so much about you, especially the media."

"It was bound to happen sooner or later. I have been thinking about going public about my book and I'm a few chapters away from finishing the sequel. Rachel and I have been talking about it. So, my life won't be private anymore. I think I am ready to finally talk about it. I will discuss the details with Rachel when we arrive in Johannesburg." I inform. I have been thinking long about this.

"That's fantastic babe," Tay says and pulls about five feet away from the big white jet written Payne Corp. We both climb out and someone takes my suitcase .

Tay holds my hand as we walk towards the small steps on the jet.

"Hailey," Tay greets and the girl gives him a small wave.

"Mr. Payne and Mrs. Payne. it is finally nice to meet you,"

"You too," I shake her hand.

"I will prepare to take off, please take your seats." She says and places her pilot hat back on her head.

"Thank you," I say, and she disappears behind a white door.

"Can I get you anything to drink sir? Ma'am?" She asks.

"Coffee," Tay says and looks at me.

"Water will be fine please," I politely smile at the blonde girl.

The girl walks away, and Tay grabs my laptop bag.

"You are working?" I ask and he nods and turns to look at me.

"Yeah, I have something that needs my attention. You should sleep. You look exhausted." He says and rubs his face in frustration.

"Are you okay? You look like you need sleep, not me," I comment, and before he can respond the girl places a coffee mug in front of Tay, and a glass and bottle of water in front of me. I don't bother using the glass. I open the bottle and take a huge gulp along with the Prep pill. I am running out.

The plane starts to move, and Tay shuts off the laptop and buckles up. Minutes later, we are in the air, and I relax in my seat closing my eyes to sleep and Tay goes back to work.

TAY

I grab the mug and take a sip. The familiar warmth travels down my throat and I sigh in relief. I glance at Olivia and find her eyes closed. I push my hair back and close my eyes at the headache forming. I have been working for the past hour and I have no fucking clue who is stealing my money or where it is. Whoever it is knew how to cover their tracks well.

I place Olivia's laptop on the small table and grab my phone. I dial Jessica's number.

She answers after the third ring.

"You know, you must stop this habit of yours of calling me at night. Some of us need our sleep so we can function in the morning." Jess says and I pull the phone away from my ear to look at the time.

"It is just past eight," I reason.

"I need more than 8 hours of sleep and you are ruining my sleep." I chuckle. She is like Olivia when it comes to sleeping.

"I have a problem,"

"Of course, you do. What is it?" She asks.

"Someone is stealing from me, and I can't seem to trace all the money. The person who did this knew what they were doing. He stole 10 million and when I outlined the money, I found only 3 million and 2 million in another account. He spread the money so it can be hard to trace. " I inform Jess.

"It looks like it is some sort of a game to me, it is like he or she is buying time but for what?" She says and I nod even though I know she can't see me.

"You think?"

"Yeah, look. The person has full access to the company accounts, and he only took 10 million. 10 million is nothing to you. You make that kind of money every two hours. If it is what I'm thinking, then this person doesn't want your money but has another motive." Jess concludes and my mind races with who could start up such a sick game messing with my company.

CHAPTER 18

OLIVIA

A hand violently shakes me, and I groan.

"Love?" A thumb caresses my cheek and I groan yet again. Lips peck my lips, and my eyes shoot open.

"We are here," Tay says and I turn my head to look at the small window. I only see the lights. I yawn and Tay scoops me in his arms taking me by surprise.

"Mr. and Mrs. Payne," Hailey says with a smile on her face and I bury my head in Tay's chest.

I lift my head off his chest and look at the city. I never thought I will be back here so soon. I thought I was leaving for good. A man in a suit opens the passenger seat for Tay and he places me on the seat and buckles me up. He jogs around the car and hops in the back seat with ne. The driver steers the car into the empty road, and I rest my head on the window and close my eyes.

"Are you okay?" Tay asks. I open my eyes and turn back to look at me.

"I don't know," I say truthfully. I only came back here because of Donald. I feel calm now, but I don't know what will happen when I go to see him.

As if he can read my mind he says, "You will be fine. I will go with you?" He offers and places his hand on my thigh.

"No, I have to do this on my own. I need to be independent. I can't always bring you with me." I say and lean my head against the seat.

"I love this brave Olivia more," I chuckle and turn to look at him.

He grabs my hand and plants a light kiss at the back of my mind and my smile grows.

"I love you,"

"I love you too," I say and look at him as he drives.

Thirty minutes later, we pulls into our house driveway, and I look at it, as I remember the last time I set foot here. I unbuckle my seatbelt and climb out of the car. Tay grabs my bag from the boot, and we walk to the front door.

The house is quiet, and we walk up the stairs to our room. Tay puts the bag down and walks to the bathroom. I grab the bag and take out my pyjamas and change. I check the time on my phone, and it reads 3 am. I get under the duvet at the same time Tay walks out of the bathroom in just pyjama pants only. He gets under the covers and pulls me closer to him. Our chests touch. His breath fans my face and we look at each other.

He brings his thumb to my face and touches my lips. I keep quiet and watch him.

"Do you think we will ever have children of our own?" I ask. I have never given myself the chance to really think about the situation.

Tay stops and continues.

"Of course, we will," he says.

"Why the question?"

"I don't know. I guess thinking of going to see Donald tomorrow just brought back memories that were caused by him." I share my thoughts and he nods in understanding.

"We will have children. Lots of them and we will live after ever happy!" He says and I chuckle and yawn.

"Sleep. You are still tired." He says and I close my eyes to sleep.

In the morning, I wake up alone on the bed. I yawn and rub my face. I climb out of the bed and lazily walk to the bathroom. I brush my teeth and take a shower. I dress up in a sweatshirt dress that ends on my mid-thighs and white sneakers and blow dry my hair.

I enter the kitchen and find Tay busy on his laptop and a mug next to the laptop.

I grab an apple from the fruit basket, and he doesn't even notice me. I take a bite and walk around the counter and to his side.

"You look stressed?" I point out when he frowns at the laptop. He jumps, a little startled.

"I didn't hear you walking in," he says and closes the laptop.

"What has you so stressed?" I ask as he places the laptop in the laptop bag.

"I will tell you in the car," he says and grabs his car keys.

I get in the passenger seat and Tay in the driver's seat. He drives into the empty road.

"I am trying to find the money that was stolen in the company accounts," Tay informs and tightens his grip on the steering wheel.

"Do you know who stole it?" I pry.

"Not yet. Every time I investigate, I reach a dead end. I don't know what to do anymore." He says and stops at a red light.

"Why don't you set a trap? and see who will fall for it. Maybe you will get the thief." I suggest.

"How?"

"I take it as the person who stole the money already knows the procedure you go through right?" Tay nods as he drives through the intersection.

"Then try something different. Don't ask me what because I also don't know. You are the one who can think like a criminal. I'm sure you will come up with something," I shrug and Tay laughs. The car comes to a halt, and I look out the window to see big prison gates staring back at me.

"Are you sure you don't want me to come with you?" He asks and I shake my head no. I take a deep breath and peck Tay on the lips and climb out of the car and watch him drive off. I walk to the gate. There is a security guard, he asks for my ID, and I show it to him. He opens the gate for me and directs me to where visitors need to go.

I join the line and when my time comes, I had over my ID and sign in. I nervously seat on the steal long chair. My palms are sweaty, and I push them down on my sweatshirt to try and calm down. I look around and take a deep breath. There are prisoners in orange overalls chattering with their families, friends, security guards walking around and warning visitors and prisoners with the 'no-touching rule'.

The sound of a door opening has me snapping my head in that direction and I lock eyes with Donald. I have only seen him in the pictures and seeing those familiar blue eyes staring back at me makes me want to get the hell out of here.

You can do it, Olivia. Just take a deep breath. My subconscious encourages.

I take a deep breath and watch as he walks in my direction. He sits across from me and keeps quiet, probably waiting for me to say something first. I open my mouth to say something but close it again not knowing what to ask him.

"Thank you for coming to see me," Donald breaks the silence and I just stare at him.

"I know what I did to you is unforgivable and I don't expect you to forgive me." He crosses his hands on the steel table.

"I didn't mean to do what I did to you, please believe me. I didn't even know what I did until the next morning. I was high on drugs that night and I still don't remember half of what happened at that party. I know no matter what I say, it won't erase what happened,"

"I first saw you at school. You were always reading a book whenever I saw you. I thought you were the most beautiful girl I had ever seen. I tried to talk to you a couple of times, but you didn't even give me the time of the day, " my eyes widen at his confession. I don't remember him.

"Your name was on every boy's lip, and you didn't even know. I am not trying to justify my actions; I am just trying to tell you that I didn't mean to hurt you. I tried to go to the police the next morning when I saw the video I took on my phone and the blood on my clothes, but David stopped me. He switched me to another school and made sure I didn't go to the police. I dedicated my life to helping women who'd suffered from men like me and I hope one day you will really find it in your heart to forgive me. I really didn't mean to hurt you, I loved you way too much to do such a thing knowingly."

CHAPTER 19

OLIVIA

I have no idea what to say or think of what Donald just dropped on me. I didn't expect him to apologize, to be honest. He is the son of David after all, and he is proving that he is not like his father.

"I am truly sorry for the pain I caused you and for not turning to the police sooner. I went away to plan everything and to avoid my father finding out what I wanted to do," he informs me, and I stare at him.

"Please say something?" He pleads.

"You know, I suffered a lot after what you did…"

"Sometimes I'd cry myself to sleep. It was the most difficult time of my life, and I had no idea how to deal with the emotions other than to shut them off. You made me feel dirty and worthless. You had control over my body, and I hated it, I couldn't even get close to a guy. I hate you for taking what didn't belong to you!" I finally say what I have been longing to say to him. What I have bottled for all those years. It's good to finally say it to his face.

"I hate you for always tormenting me in my dreams. I hate you so much and I wish you never get out!" I yell and wipe my tears. I look at him and find him already looking at me with a look I can't read. I feel like I can ultimately breath after so many years of struggling. I have always imagined how it would be talking to him—telling him how I feel and the hate he put inside my heart.

"I understand. I don't expect you to forgive me. I am at peace now that I am paying for what I did." He says and gives me a small smile making me feel guilty for telling him how much I hate his guts.

"Time is up!" a security guard yells, and I look at Donald one more time, grab my bag and walk to the door with other visitors.

I sign out and walk out of the prison. I walk down the road trying to gather my thoughts and feelings. I have no idea what I am feeling or what I should feel. Seeing Donald wasn't what I imagined. I expected him to brag at my face, tell me how good it was to have his way with me, that he is not sorry, and he doesn't regret a thing. I didn't expect an apology.

A car honk breaks me from my train of thoughts, and I look at the road to find a taxi. I point my finger down and it stops in front of me. I open the backseat door and hop in.

"Payne Corporation," I tell the driver and he drives into the less busy road. I open my phone and see Future's missed call. Tay must have told her that I am back. It has been a while since I saw her. I dial her number and she answers on the first ring.

"Hey!"

"Oh my God! it is good to hear your voice again. Is it true that you are back?"

"Yes, but not for good. I just came to do something. " I tell her and hear a cry from the background.

"Is that Eric?" I ask with a smile playing on my lips.

"Yes, I am feeding him. I wanted to ask if you would be able to meet up before you leave?" She asks.

"Yes, of course."

"Great! You will tell me when you are free?"

"Yeah," We talk for a while and hang up when the taxi comes to a halt in front of the Payne Corporation building.

"Thanks," I tell the driver and climb out of the car.

I walk inside the building and walk to the receptionist table. The same girl from the first time I came here is standing behind the desk.

"Hi, I am here to see Tay," her eyes widen and look for something on her desk.

"Yes, you can go up Mrs. Payne." She says nervously and I pull my lower lip between my teeth to keep a laugher from coming out. I walk to the elevator and step in with other staff members. I stand at the back as I listen to their gossip.

"The boss is back, I saw him this morning and he looked really pissed," one says holding a blue file.

"I heard that someone stole from the company. Whoever did it must have a death wish." another one says, and I keep quiet.

"Nah! I bet he didn't get laid last night that's why he is so grumpy today," I choke on my own breath and keep my head from their eyes. If Tay heard what they are saying about him right now he would surely fire them all. The elevators beep open, and they all step out leaving me in the elevator all by myself.

The elevator beeps open after a while, and I step out.

"Is Tay in?" I ask the girl outside Tay's office.

"Yes," she says, and I knock and open the door. Tay is sitting on his chair with a laptop in front of him. He signals for me to enter and I walk around his table and sit on his lap.

"Hey!" I peck his lips with my hands around his neck.

"You are in a good mood?" He raises his eyebrow at me questioningly.

"Seeing you got me in a good mood," I say and run my fingers through his hair.

"Oh yeah!" He says seductively and a smile breaks on my lips.

"Yes, and I bet this table is strong is enough to hold us," I say seductively and Tay smirks.

"You don't say," his smirk is cruel like he knows something I don't.

"Uhm, sir! I think we should continue this another time," a voice says from behind and I jump off Tay's lap turning around to face multiple eyes on me on the laptop.

"How... How long have they been watching!"

"Since the beginning,"

"Fuck me!" I get off his lap and run to the bathroom and Tay laughs.

CHAPTER 20

OLIVIA

"How did it go with Donald?" Tay asks when I walk out of the bathroom.

I keep quiet and walk to the creamy couch.

"Are you angry at me?" He asks, amused and I wish I could knock his smirk off.

"Do you how humiliating that was?" I ask and glare at him. He laughs and walks to the couch.

"It's not my fault that you didn't check if I had a meeting or not. You have yourself to blame for what happened," he shrugs his shoulders like it's nothing.

"How are you feeling?" His tone changes to a worried one and my insides melt at his caring side.

"I am fine," I say, and he lifts me up and places me on his lap.

"Are you sure?"

"Yes, I am sure." I laugh because this is weird right now. We spent half of our time hurting each other rather than taking care of each other.

"How was it, seeing him?" Tay asks and tucks a strand of my hair behind my ear. He loves doing that, says he loves to get a full view of my face. I wrap my hands around his neck to support myself.

"At first I thought I won't be able to do it and for a moment I regretted coming back—but a part of me wanted to do this," I say as he draws circles on mh hand with his finger—submitting the comfort he knows how to offer.

"A part that was tired of the nightmares, feeling like dirt, feeling insecure, and worthless did it and I have you to thank. You have done more than you can think for me and for that, you are my hero, my saviour." I kiss his nose and he gives me a warm smile.

"You never gave up on me—on us. Heaven knows how much we have suffered but you still fought against people and the universe that wanted to separate us. Your love gave me the strength to keep on going—to keep on fighting because I had something to live for. You gave me purpose and you will be my end. I will never be able to give someone else my heart because it's yours. I am yours body, mind, and soul." I say and Tay looks at me with a look he has never looked at me with.

"Our faith in our love was tested so many times and we kept fighting—we climbed mountains after mountains, and we finally moved them aside. I love you so fucking much now, tomorrow, and forever. You are the strongest woman I have ever met in my entire life; you are an inspiration to women out there, living proof of what survival is all about. You taught me to fight no matter how bad a situation gets, and I love you so much for that. The world has found its next Maya Angelou," Tay's forehead is on mine—looking deep into my soul.

"I love you," I tell him, and he pecks my lips.

I never imagined myself with Tay or a family when I first met him, I didn't even know how it was like to fall in love, how to love— how you act around the person, I was clueless. Never in my life will I ever fall for someone. He fought for me— for our love and I don't know what would have happened to us if he didn't.

"Did you hear me?" Tay asks, shaking me and I blink twice at him.

"What?"

"I asked if you wanted to go home?" I nod and get off his lap. I grab my bag and he grabs his laptop bag and car keys—and we walk out.

We step in a private elevator and Tay presses the ground level. After a while, the elevator peeps open, and we step out. We walk to his car, and I hop in the passenger seat, and he walks to the driver's seat. He drives into the busy road of Sandton, and I rest my head against the window.

A hand caresses my cheek and I open my eyes to find Tay in my view.

"We are home," he says, and my lips form a smile. I unbuckle my seatbelt and hop out of the car.

We walk inside the house, and I throw myself on the couch. Tay chuckles and sits next to me and lifts my legs —and places them on his lap. He takes off my shoes and massages my foot.

"The house is quiet, " I comment.

"Yeah, it is." He agrees and continues to massage my foot. I let out a grunt and a doorbell rings. I groan when Tay stops and walks to the door. I lift myself from the couch to look at the person at the door and my eyes almost bulge out of their sockets.

"Dad!" I get up from the couch.

"So, it is true?" Dad ignores Tay and walks in.

"What are you talking about?" I ask, confused.

"That my daughter is back and didn't even tell me—let alone let me know that she is going to visit the person who ruined her life!" He says with hurt in his eyes.

"And let's not forget she got back with the person who is related to the person who ruined her,"

"Dad I—"

"No Olivia! I am not going to sit and watch my daughter ruin her life more than it is already ruined!" He yells.

"Don't talk to her like that! Didn't you bail out on her at the hospital when she needed you?" Tay asks Dad and I pinch the bridge of my nose in frustration.

"Don't tell me how to talk to my daughter kid, I watched my daughter's life get ruined in front of me and I didn't do shit—but I won't this time. You and I both know that you don't deserve her. She needs someone who respects her and doesn't constantly hurt her little heart." Dad says, glaring at Tay.

"Joe, I know you don't like me because of what Donald did to Olivia but I love your daughter and I will do anything for her to be happy even if her happiness lies with someone else—but your daughter loves me, and I'm done with people telling us what we should do and shouldn't. You must accept that we love each other and there's nothing you could do about it. I am not Donald, and I will never be him, but I am not perfect. I will hurt Olivia and she will hurt me, that's how life is. I understand you are looking out for your daughter, and I respect that—I really do but you also must respect us. Olivia is not a kid anymore, she made her choice and that's to stay with me and I hope you will find it in your heart to respect her decisions and choices as her father," he tells dad and a smile forms on my lips.

CHAPTER 21

OLIVIA

"Dad, I really don't want to fight with you. As Tay said, I chose him and I expect you to respect my decisions." I say and Tay gives me a million-dollar smile. I know dad was shocked and hurt when he found out my past and I don't blame him for not wanting me to get back with Tay, but he also bailed out on me in Cape Town.

"I guess I don't have a choice than to respect your decisions. I hope you know what you are doing Olivia because I don't want you to get hurt again. I am not going to lie and say I'm happy because I'm not. You have suffered so much at a young age, life hasn't been fair to you, and I hope that you get all the happiness in the world that you are seeking for," dad says and my heart melts at his words.

"I am happy dad!" I walk to him and take both of his hands in mine.

"I appreciate you looking out for me. It makes me happy that you care but I promise I am happy. There is no person in this world that can make me happy like Tay does I promise," I say, and dad gives me a smile.

TAY

I watch as Olivia hugs her dad and I smile proudly of her for standing up for us. I am the happiest man on the planet right now. Olivia and Joe sit in the living room and I pad the stairs to our room. I strip out of my suit and get into jeans and a t-shirt. My phone rings when I walk out of the bathroom. Jessica's name flashes on the screen and I answer.

"Hey?" I say putting my tennis shoes on.

"I have good news for you!" I sit up straight leaving my shoes unfinished.

"I am listening…" I push my hair off my forehead.

"I know who stole the money and it's the last person you will ever suspect in your entire life," she says.

"Who?" I ask quickly.

"I can't tell you on the phone. Let's meet at the Connie cafe?"

"Okay, I will be there in 30 minutes!" I say and hang up. I grab my phone and walk out of the room.

I enter the kitchen to find Olivia handing her dad a plate of food and I walk behind and wrap my arm around her, and she leans back to me.

"Should I warn him to put the hospital number on speed dial!" I ask. She lets out a giggle and it's the best giggle ever. I love seeing her like this and I hope everything stays like this forever.

"Technically I didn't prepare the food! He just told me what to do and where to put stuff so if something goes wrong then it's his fault!" She whispers and I bite back a laugh. I won't mind ending up in the hospital because of her food poisoning but for others...

"We are going have to get some cooking lessons," I say as I watch Joe eat his food.

"Are you going somewhere?" She asks and turns around and looks at me.

"Yeah, I have to meet with Jessica about the theft case," I tell her and tuck her hair behind her ear.

"Do you want to come with me?"

"No, I promised my father that we will spend the day together." She informs and hums in response.

"Doing what?" I pry.

"He hasn't said anything yet, but I will text you if we leave the house,"

"Okay, love you" I peck her lips.

"Joe?" I nod at him and walk to the front door.

30 minutes later, I drive my car into the connie cafe lot and climb out. I walk to the small cafe and push the door open and walk-in. I look around and Jess lifts her hand in the air, and I walk to her.

"So, who is it?" I ask as I slid into the booth.

"What? No how are doing Jess?"

"Jess?" I warn and a smile breaks.

"Okay fine! Where is your sense of humour?" She hands me her phone.

"I don't do sense of humour," I say and click on the video. I watch the video from the beginning not believing my eyes.

"What the—"

"Yeah, it is shocking. Out of all people it had to be him."

"But how? Why?" I ask no one in particular. I can suspect many people but him. It is so unlike him.

"What are you going to do now?" Jess asks. I hand her back her phone and lean back on the booth.

"How did you find out? Because when I checked it was erased from the database?" I ask avoiding her question because I don't know what to do. My mind is still processing what it is I just saw.

"It was erased from the database but there was another camera that he didn't see. It was well hidden purposely for this kind of stuff." She says and takes a sip from her chocolate milkshake.

"Let's go?" I say grabbing my car keys.

"Where?"

"His place," I say and place the milkshake bill on the table. We walk out of the cafe and walk to my car.

"Where is your car?" I ask as I hop in the driver's seat.

"I came here with a taxi," I drive into the busy highway.

"You haven't told me what you are going to do?"

"That's because I don't know," I say, and my phone buzzes. I grab it and open the message from Olivia.

Went out with my father to watch a game. I almost let out a laugh because I know Olivia knows nothing about soccer.

I drive into the house lot and we both climb out. I place my phone back in my back pocket and walk to the front door. I knock and wait. The door opens revealing Danny.

"Boss?" He questions.

"Why the fuck did you steal from me?"

"What!" Danny says shocked and I push past him and walk to the living room.

"You heard me, why did you steal from me?" I sit on a single couch and cross my legs.

"I don't know what you are talking about, I would—"

"Don't insult me, please. You know exactly what I am talking about. Do not irritate me further . "

"I didn't mean to do it," he says quickly. His voice is weak and sounds like he is about to cry.

Pathetic.

"But you did it anyway. I cannot believe I continued to give you chances when you messed up my deals! I should have seen it sooner. Who sent you?" I stare at him, and he squirms under my intense gaze.

"I picked you off the street and fed you and you have the nerve to steal from me?" I stand up from the couch and walk to him. I place both of my hands on either side of his single couch and look at him in the eyes.

"This is the last time I am going to ask you, Who. Sent. You?" I ask.

"I.... I don't know," he cries out and my hand goes to his neck and squeezes the life out of him.

"Who the fuck sent you?" I yell and Danny cries trying to pry my hand away from his neck and I squeeze harder.

"Fuck Tay! You will kill him!" Jess tries to get me to let go but I am already far in deep.

"Who the fuck sent you?" I yell and take my hand off when his eyes start to close.

He coughs holding his neck while tears ran down his neck. I push my hair off my face and watch him.

"I swear I don't know." He informs.

"And you expect me to believe that!"

"Yes, I have no idea who hired me. I didn't want to do it, but they threatened me with my family. They still have them," he cries.

"I haven't seen them in months. They took them away from me and said I have to do what they tell me or else I will never see my wife and kids again." He informs and I watch him not knowing what to believe.

"How do we know that you are telling the truth?" Jess asks.

"I have.... I have a video and pictures they sent me. They are in my drawer in my room." He says and Jess walks out of the living room to get them.

"I never meant to betray you, boss. I swear on my family's life, but I had no choice. I had to save them," he cries, and a small part feels for him because I know what he means. somehow, I can relate to him. I would do anything for Olivia even if it meant dying for her. I would do it in a heartbeat.

"Found them," Jess says walking in.

"He is telling the truth, "

"Why didn't you come to me?" I ask him.

"I couldn't. They knew my every move and one mistake they could have killed my wife."

"The money you stole? "

"I don't know much about it. They just gave me accounts to transfer to. They just gave out orders and I didn't ask questions." He informs and I nod. What I found hard to believe is why they would put the money in an account I would find so easy.

"The deals?"

"It was on their orders to sabotage them. I tried to tell you on time so that you can be able to save them." He informs and I stare at him with no emotion.

"Tell whoever hired you that I will find him and when I do, hell will break loose." I spat and walks to the front door. I meant what I told Danny; whoever he is I will find him.

I hop in the driver's seat and wait for Jess to get in and when she does, I drive away.

"What now?" Jess asks.

"I want you to focus on this case, find those fuckers." I answer.

"Olivia's birthday and Valentine's day are coming up in two days, so I want to do something for her," I tell her and stop at a red light.

"Oh!" Jess says and I turn to look at her, but her head is turned to the window. She couldn't possibly still have feelings for me, could she? The light turns green, and I pass the intersection.

CHAPTER 22

OLIVIA

I miss Tay terribly, but I promised dad that I will spend time with him which I regret now. He took me to a soccer game. I know nothing about soccer but the smile on his face prevents me from telling him. He took me to watch Pirates and Chief's playing and so far, both teams haven't scored. From what I have heard both teams suck but people still support them. Talk about loyalty.

"Goal!" I snap my eyes from my phone to watch my dad screaming and Pirates celebrating. It is so weird watching him like this.

Thirty minutes later, the match ends, and we walk out of the stadium.

"Where do you want to go?" He asks as we walk to his car.

"I am tired. I just want to go home if you don't mind?" I ask as I check the time on my phone.

"Of course," he says, and I get in the passenger seat. I don't have any missed calls from Tay.

"Nora is happy that you are back, you should make time to visit her," Dad says as he drives me home.

"I will but I am not back for good. Tay and I have decided to stay in Cape Town. He is busy opening a branch there." I inform Dad.

"Oh! That's good. Have you guys found a house yet?" He asks.

"We want a house built from scratch. He arranged for us to meet his architect." I tell Dad and put my phone in my bag.

"Isn't that expensive?"

"Tell that to Tay," I laugh.

He pulls into the house driveway and Tay's car is already parked.

"Thank you for today," I say and kiss him on the cheek and hop out.

I walk to the front door and open it. I walk into the smell of steak. I make my way to the kitchen to find Tay taking the steak out of the oven.

"Hey!" I say and he turns and pecks my lips.

"Hey you're back!" he laughs.

"I missed you!" I confess and hug his back.

He turns around and wraps his hands on my waist.

"I missed you more," he pecks my lips again.

"I made dinner, "

"I can see that," I take a seat on the barstool and he hands me a glass of white wine and a plate with medium rare steak on it.

"How was your day?" He asks as he pours himself a glass of wine.

"It was eventful," I say and take a sip from my glass.

"And yours?" I ask.

"Worse," he says and takes a seat next to me.

***

I wake up to an empty bed and water running in the shower. I push my hair off my face and roll off the bed. I walk to the bathroom and spot Tay in the shower. I strip out of my clothes and step into the shower.

I kiss his back and he turns to look at me.

"Hey!" He pecks my lips and I wrap my hands around his neck and deepen the kiss. His hands go to my waist and pull me closer. I slip my tongue in his mouth and he lets out a moan. I can feel butterflies forming in the pit of my stomach and I tug the roots of his hair. I can never get over a kiss from him.

He breaks the kiss and rests his forehead on mine.

"I have to go to the office," he says, still panting. I ignore him and trail kisses down his chest going down. I snap my head up to look at him but already find his on me with curiosity and excitement. This is the second time I am going to suck his member, but I feel nervous like the first time. I kneel in front of him and take his length in my hand. He is hard as a rock.

"Fuck!" He says when I lick the tip of his head.

"You look so good on your knees ready to take me whole," he comments making my sex throb more than it already has. I take him in both of my hands and stroke him up and down, he groans and pushes his hair back as water cascades on our bodies. I take him in my mouth and his hands run into my hair. I suck him while stroking him where my mouth can't take him, and he grabs a fistful of my hair and I grip on his thighs as he assaults my mouth.

The bathroom is filled with groans, running water, and moans.

"Fuck! Your mouth feels so good," he says, and he fills my mouth with his seed, and I swallow all of it. He pulls out and before I can say anything he turns me around against the glass shower wall and enters me from behind. A loud moan escapes from my mouth.

"I love how tight you feel every time I bury myself inside you," he whispers in my ear and a shiver runs down my spine. He grabs my arms and pulls them back and pounds into me. I roll my eyes at the back of my head in pleasure. He feels so deep and full inside me that it's hard to control the pressure building in the pit of my stomach.

"Yes!" I moan and throw my head back.

"Fuck!" He lets go of my arms and wraps his hand on my torso and the other one on my neck and he pulls me closer to his body. I can feel his breath on my neck as he pounds into my heat like an animal, and I lift my hands to his hair.

"I love you," he says into my ear as he increases his stride hitting the deepest corners of my walls.

"I... love...you...so fucking...much. Oh, fuck!" He takes one last pound that sends both of us into an intense climax. My body automatically falls against the shower wall, and he follows but keeps his palms on the wall to lift off his weight on me.

"Fuck! That was intense," I nod my head yes as my breathing hasn't come back to normal.

"I love you," I turn around to look at him and he pushes my wet hair off my face. I watch as water cascades down his face and he does not attempt to wipe.

"We need to have morning sex often, God! That was beautiful." I laugh and he lifts himself off me.

"I am seriously late for a meeting," Tay says as he helps wash my hair.

"They will understand," I chuckle.

"What are your plans for today?" He asks as I dry myself.

"I am meeting up with Future at the mall to catch up."

"Okay, I will leave the card for you, and this time please don't argue with me? It makes me feel kind of useless when you don't use my money, " he confesses while drying his hair and I turn to look at him.

"Why didn't you say anything?"

"Because I didn't want to sound like I was taking over your life and controlling it," a smile forms on my lips at the frown on his face. I stand in front of him and wrap my hands around his neck.

"I love you, " I tell him, and a smile forms on his lips.

"What did I do to deserve you?" He asks.

"I have been asking myself the same question too," before he can respond, a phone ringing interrupts him. He pecks my lips and walks out of the bathroom. I finish drying myself and walk out to find Tay dressing up.

"What happened?"

"I am super late for a meeting," he says and grabs his laptop bag.

"Love you," with that he walks out. I shake my head and walk to the wardrobe. I dress up in jeans and a blue sweater.

I grab my bag and walk out. I enter the kitchen and grab a banana and walk out.

I dial Futures number and she answers on the first ring.

"Hey!"

"Hi," I say as I walk down the neighborhood's street.

" I am free if you still want to meet?"

"Yes! Where?"

"Rosebank mall?" I suggest and she agrees and hangs up. I continue my walk and stop a taxi after a while.

Thirty minutes later, I am at the mall, and we meet at Edgars and buy a few dresses with Tay's black card.

We make our way to King Pie and place orders.

"Hey little guy," I pinch Eric's cheekbones. He is so adorable.

"I feel like I haven't seen you in like forever!" Future says as I slide in the booth.

I laugh.

"So, I want you to help me with my wedding!"

"Me?" I point a finger at myself.

"Yes, what is wrong with you helping me?"

"I don't know a damn thing about planning a wedding," I state the obvious

"Come on, pretty please? You are the only one I can think of who can help and advise me, "

"What about a wedding planner?" I ask as a waiter places a tray with our pies on our table.

"I don't want a wedding planner. Please, Olivia?" She takes my hands in hers.

"Okay! Fine." I give in and she squeals. We spend the next 3 to 4 hours at the mall shopping for Eric and I get Tay some t-shirts and watches. He loves wearing them with suits.

When I get home, it is around 6 pm.

"Hey!" I peck his lips.

"I spoke to the architects, and he sent a picture of the design, do you want to see it?" I nod and Tay opens his laptop and turns it.

"I bought a land close to the beach in Cape Town to build it. It's quiet, " he informs.

"Don't you think 8 rooms is quite a big number?" I ask.

"I don't think so, we might have eight children," he says, and I laugh. The plan has 8 rooms, a living room, a kitchen, a study, and a movie room.

"When will the house get built?"

"As soon as you approve the plan," he informs, and I nod.

"I love it, you can give them a go-ahead," he smiles and pecks my lips.

My phone rings when I walk into the room and I answer,

"Hello?"

"Hey! Do you still want to come out? About the book and you know?" Rachel asks.

"Yes, "

"Great! I will get you an interview with one of my friend's studios, "

"Okay, did you get a chance to look for a publicist for me?"

"Yes, you will meet him tomorrow if you want?"

"I can..." Tay kisses my neck and Rachel's voice becomes distant.

"Tay, I am on the phone?"

"Rachel will understand," he says and continues to kiss my neck and I let out a moan.

"Okay, I think I am going to hang up. Don't want..." Tay grabs my phone and throws it on the couch. He turns me around and attacks my lips. I wrap my hands around his neck, he hoists me up and I wrap my legs around his waist.

"Fuck! I can never get enough of you," he says and sits down on the bed with me on his lap.

I help him take off his t-shirt and crash our lips together. This time the kiss is fast, rough, and passionate. He takes off my shirt and grabs my breasts causing me to throw my head back in pleasure.

"You are so beautiful," he says seductively. My hands go to his shorts, and he gets up. I stand in front of him as he takes off his shorts. He takes off my pants and turns me around. He wraps his arm around me and pulls me back. He sits down on the bed and adjusts me on his length and a moan comes out.

"Fuck! I am in love, " he says.He opens his legs wider and pounds into me. His arm moves to my breast, and I throw my head back moaning. He pounds faster, deeper, and rough.

"Oh!" I moan out and he places sloppy kisses on my bare shoulder.

"You look sexy getting fucked," sweat covers all our bodies and it's a beautiful sight to see.

He holds my body tight and pounds into me like a crazy animal. I can feel the pressure building in the pit of my stomach.

"Tay!" My wall clenches around him and he releases his seed inside me. My back falls back into his chest and he pulls me ever closer to him.

"I am addicted to you, your body, and everything that you do," He pulls out and we stand up and walk to the bathroom to take a quick shower and go to bed.

The next morning, I wake up alone on the bed. I grab Tay's t-shirt and walk out. I hear music walking down the stairs. I enter the kitchen to find Tay cooking shirtless.

After a while, he turns and smiles at me

"Do you have a dress?" Tay asks.

"Uhm, yes. Why?"

"Just want to do something for you," he says.

"Okay?" I finish.

The days goes by quickly and now I am preparing for tonight. I finish curling my hair at the end and dress up in a crisp monochrome pleated flare dress. I put on my heels, grab a purse, and walk out.

I find Tay waiting for me at the door with flowers. I pull my lower lip between my teeth to stop a laugh from coming out. He looks so cute holding flowers.

"Happy birthday and happy valentine my love," he hands me flowers. This is the first time he gave me flowers.

"Thank you,"

I place the flowers in a vase, and we walk out. He holds my hand as we walk to the car.

Minutes later we park in front of a restaurant.

He opens the door for me and there are red petals on the floor, and a round table in the middle.

"Mr. Payne welcome," a voice says, and I turn to find Tay shaking a young man's hand.

"You rented this whole place?" I ask when I notice there are no people here.

"Yes, come." he places his hand on my back and we walk to the table. A waiter places plates in front of us and glasses.

After desert, Tay asks me to dance.

"You are kidding right?" I laugh.

"No," he says, grabbing my hand, and music starts.

"This is crazy," I comment. He lets go of my hand and kneels in front of me.

"What are you doing?" I ask while laughing. He takes out a red valet box and reveals a ring. My eyes widen.

"You married me because you were forced. You are the strongest woman I have ever met in my life, and I love you so much. I know I have hurt you more than I could count, and I promise I will spend the rest of my life making it up to you. We tried to stay away from each other, but we ended up in each other's arms. We belong together. We are allergic to other people; you are the one for me. I want you to marry me because you love me this time so, Olivia Payne will you please marry me, again?" He asks and I wipe my tears.

I nod my head yes and he gets up and turns me around

CHAPTER 23

OLIVIA

"It's beautiful," I comment when we walk into our car. I still can't believe that he proposed! It feels so surreal.

"Where are we going?"

"You will see,"

"Is Nate coming back for the wedding?" I ask. To be honest I miss him and his sweet jokes.

"Yeah, he called me in the morning that he is in Johannesburg," he informs me.

We pull up in front of the club and we climb out.

"What are we doing here?"

"Patience."

We walk in and make our way to the VIP section.

"Surprise!" I smile at the familiar faces.

"Nate!" I hug him first.

"Happy birthday sister-in-law!" he says handing me a glass and I don't bother asking what it is. Future, Andrew, Jessica, Rachel are here, and this is the best way to celebrate a birthday, with family and friends.

TAY

Olivia is happy and I am happy but not with the fact that Nate is busy giving her glass after glass of booze.

"Nate?" I warn.

"Come on brother. Aren't you curious drunk Olivia? Because I am!"

"Fine."

Some song blasts through the room the girls scream.

I watch as Olivia dances and sings along which I didn't know she could do.

The girls sing.

The whole club has gone into crazy mode.

Olivia gets on the table and starts dancing holding the red wine bottle and to say it's a rare and funny sight to see is an understatement.

"Yes! Show them how it's done!" Nate yells laughing like never before and taking a video.

Olivia starts to unzip her dress and I rush to her.

"Time to go!"

"No!" I lift her over my shoulder

"Booze in the air!" she yells over the music

"Shake what your mama gave you!"

"Highlight of my whole life!" Nate laughs.

I manage to get out of the club and the driver opens the backseat door and we climb in.

"Take us home please," I tell the driver.

"Music driver!" she demands.

"I think you have had enough dancing love," she doesn't listen and rolls down the window when music plays.

"It's my birthday bitches!" she yells through the window

"Cheers to life!'

"Okay. Get back inside before you get hurt!"

Minutes later, the car pulls up at our house and I carry her inside.

"I don't want to sleep," she whines.

"I can tell but you have to," I say and after an hour of trying to get her to sleep she finally settles down and I can breathe again.

CHAPTER 24

OLIVIA

The next morning, I wake up alone on the bed. I groan and roll off the bed to the bathroom and take a shower.

I find Tay in the kitchen. He hands me a glass of water and a pill. I don't ask and take it as my head hurts.

"What's wrong?" He asks, tucking my hair behind my ear.

"Don't let me drink again." I rest my forehead on his chest, and he continues to hold me.

"Do you remember what you did last night?" He asks, with a smile.

"No! I want to go back to sleep," I run back upstairs.

TAY

My phone rings as Olivia runs upstairs.

"Jess?" I answer.

"Hey, how is everything going?"

"What did you find out?"

"I honestly don't know what is true or what's not, "

"What do you mean?"

"It looks like this is deeper. I had to go back to Andrews's mother's case. Remember the half-brother he has that no one knows or has seen his face?" I nod but remember she cannot see me.

"Yes?"

"It's him but there is more,"

"I am listening,"

"When last did you see Chad Brown?" she asks, shocking me.

"I don't know but it can't be him, Jess. He buried his mother. It's impossible." I argue.

"But what are the chances that he is the half-brother we have been looking for? And he has been right under our nose?" She reasons but I shake my head no.

"It can't be," I repeat.

"He has been AWOL and suddenly your company is suffering! Come on."

"We don't have proof that he is Andrews's half-brother."

"Okay, if you say so." She says and hangs up. My mind is racing. I don't know what to think right now. Chad may be a lot of things but this? I disagree. I know him and I at least would have known if he was Andrew's half-brother. He had a mother growing up so it's impossible for him to be Andrew's half-brother. They don't even look alike. I push my hair back frustrated with all the theories.

I place my phone on the coffee table and check on Olivia. I find her asleep, and I take off my shoes and slip in the duvet facing her. I tuck her hair behind her ear and watch her.

"I love you," I say and continue to look at her. She looks so innocent sleeping and like a girl that hasn't seen the harshness of the world but, she has defeated it.

I peck her lips and close my eyes to sleep.

CHAPTER 25

OLIVIA

Two days have passed by as a blur since the incident at the club and I had back-to-back interviews. Everyone knows who wrote Behind Closed Doors and that the sequel is coming soon. I had to open an Instagram and Twitter page in Rachel's words. I got millions of followers within a week and that blew my mind away. A lot of DMs about how they love me and how much I have changed their lives. It is so crazy, and I had to help Future with her wedding. We managed to find a venue and she designed her wedding dress. It's so beautiful that she wants to open a boutique selling wedding dresses and this will be her big break into the industry. The venue is not big since Future wants a small intimate wedding with friends and family. We managed to get Sofia to agree to cater for the wedding under short notice. I have never worked under pressure in my entire life as I did two days ago.

Tay and I have been so busy with our work, he comes back tired from work, and I am also tired from planning the wedding.

"For fucks sake!" A voice brings me out of my train of thoughts, and I look at Rachel trying to cover her body. I follow her line sight and see Nate shutting the door behind him.

"Oh, come on! It's not like I haven't seen anything," I chuck a shoe at him, and he tucks down in time, and the shoe hits the door.

"It's the women's dressing room you idiot. Don't you know how to read?" He ignores me and stands in front of the mirror fixing his tux.

"You look beautiful by the way, sister-in-law," he says and winks at me, ignoring Rachel who is waiting for his compliment.

"What are you doing here Nate?" Future walks out of the bathroom and almost yells when she sees Nate.

"What the—"

"Will you ladies chill out? I got tired of Andrew and Tay sob pep talk. Like you would bet he is going to have a kidney transplant!" I smack the back of his head and he swears.

"Really! Sister-in-law? What did I do?"

"You need to go," Future tells Nate.

"Please don't send me back there! It's so depressing!" A chuckle escapes my lips.

"Then take Eric with you, I'm sure Kyle won't mind entertaining you," Future puts baby Eric in Nates hands and opens the door for him.

"But—" Future gently pushes him out before he can finish his sentence.

"He is a pain in the ass," she says, and I laugh and help her into her wedding dress. Her make up is on point and she looks beautiful.

"How do I look?" She asks and turns around.

"You look beautiful," I smile brightly at her.

TAY

This is the moment I am fucking proud of my little brother. I may not say it to him but I am. I am happy to see him getting ready for his own wedding. Our parents may not be here with us, but I am here to support him. To be his brother, mother, and dad at the same time. Joe left to check on Nora and as for Nate, you can never know. I just hope he is not causing trouble wherever he is.

The door opens and Nate walks in with Eric in his hand and Kyle walking closely behind. I am sure both Andrew and I jaw dropped to the floor at what we were witnessing.

1. Because Nate hates kids, I mean he loathes children and anything to do with them.

He walks straight to me and settles Eric into my arms.

"Here is your monster nephew,"

"Why do you have Eric?" I ask and try to get him to stop crying.

"Well, you might need to sit down for this one," he says looking at Andrew and he sits down looking confused. I was sure that I mirrored him.

"I need you to be calm when I tell—"

"Nate!" I warn.

"Okay! Future ran away," he blurts out and my heart quickens, worried for Andrew.

"What?" Andrew stands up.

"I told you to be calm, "

"Don't tell me what to do," he yells and runs his hand through his hair.

"Did she tell you why? Did she leave a note or something?" He looks at Nate with a pleading look.

"Well, she said that she cannot do this anymore, that she was crazy to even think of marrying you. You ruined her life and that your family is crazy, and she cannot handle it—" Nate gets cut off by the door opening and Nora walks in.

"What's going on?" She asks as she looks between us.

"Why did you let Future leave?" Andrew asks and she frowns.

"What are you talking about?" She asks and I notice Nate backing away from us and walking towards the door.

That dipshit!

"That Future ran away, "

"Huh? Who told you such nonsense?"

"I wouldn't open that door If I were you," I warn him, and Nate turns around with a smile on his face. I place Eric in Nora's arms.

"I'm sorry okay! But you guys were too serious like we are in a f—" Andrew launches at Nate and I quickly get between them.

"Andrew!" I warn him.

"I swear to God when I get my hands on you I wi …"

"You won't do anything, "

"It's done," a small voice says, and my eyes move to a small voice beside Nora. Kyle is holding a phone and it seems like he was taking a video.

"You are so easy to mess with!" With that Nate bolts out the door laughing, and I pull my lower lip between my teeth to conceal my laugh.

"I will fucking kill him!" he growls and Kyle laughs.

We finish dressing up and I have to get Andrew and Nate away from killing each other most of the time.

"Do you think she will show up?" Andrew asks as we are waiting for the bride and bridesmaids to show up.

"Nah, " Nate says and I glare at him to shut up.

"Of course, she will, don't listen to this dipshit. You know how much he hates commitments, " I never understood Nate's hate for commitments. He hates being tied down to one person and I sometimes wondered how him, and Rachel ended up together. I feel sorry for the poor woman because if she is expecting Nate to marry her then she is in for a huge surprise.

Music starts and Andrew sighs, a smile appearing on his lips, and I watch as Jess, Rachel, and my Olivia walk towards us with bright smiles on their faces. I mouth 'I love you' when Olivia passes me. Seconds later Joe walks in with Future. She looks so beautiful, and it was so beautiful of Joe to agree to walk Future down the aisle. My eyes move around the people in the church. Nora is sitting in the front row seat with Eric in her arms. Kyle besides Shawn, Kyles's mother, and that dipshit doctor that wants Olivia. And the rest of Futures friends from college and Andrews friends that I haven't met.

Joe hands Future to Andrew and goes to sit down beside Nora. I listen to Andrew and Future say their vows to each other and after what felt like forever the priest pronounces them wife and husband. We all cheer for them and make our way to the receptionist.

We ate and danced; everything was just perfect. We were all happy, my brother was married and happy.

"Did I tell you how gorgeous you look tonight?" I say into Olivia's ear and hear a sharp breath leave her lips. I love how easily I can get her so worked up with desire.

"No," she says, her eyes on the dance floor and before we can continue our little tease, Nate interrupts.

"I haven't danced like that in a while," he says panting and I lean back against my glass chair.

"Did I interrupt something?" He asks, eyeing us and I shrug. Kyle grabs Olivia by the hand and drags her off.

"Watch out," Andrew says sitting with us on the round table pointing to the dance floor. Women are gathered around, and Rachel is also with them waiting for Future to throw her flowers. We watch as the flowers go in Rachel's direction and her hands reaching out.

"Oh no! No, no, no, no!" The flowers end up in Rachels hands and Nate bangs his head on the table and we laugh.

So much for not the commitment guy!

"Have you guys seen Kyle?" Shawn asks, worried.

"I have been looking for him for the past half an hour," he says pushing his hair back.

"Now that you are saying, it's been a while since I saw him or Olivia" Jessica says, looking worried.

"We will help look," we all stand up and walk in different directions. I look in the food sections and under the table for Kyle but don't find him. A scream coming from the direction of the restroom had us running in that direction.

I find Jessica frozen, her body shaking and others approaching from behind. I stop in my tracks when I see Kyles's phone crashed and a small pool of blood on the floor. None of us say anything, our breath caught in our throats.

My phone rings in my pocket startling me. I take it out and answer.

"Miss me, little nephew?" The voice of the man I thought I will never hear says, and my blood runs cold.

"Missing Someone there? or should I say two someone's?"

"You fucking—"

"Call the cops and your little wife and the kid are dead," he hangs up and I throw the phone away.

Fucking David and how the hell did he get out of jail!

CHAPTER 26

TAY

The last time I was this scared was when I found my sister in her own pool of blood. I haven't said a word since I found the phone and blood on the floor. Many scenarios are running in my mind, and I don't know which one could be it, but what I am most scared about is Kyle. He is just a kid, innocent and now he is in the hands of a psychopath. I know Olivia is strong.

"How the hell did David escape? And how am I hearing this now?"

I called one of the trusted cops and made sure the media was left out of it, and it turns out David escaped. He made the police believe that he was seriously sick, and they took him to the hospital yesterday where he escaped.

"We were going to tell you," The detective I learned is Jessica's friend says. Shawn hasn't stopped pacing. He is trying to be strong, but I know he is hurting.

"Your negligence caused Kyle, a kid who has a heart problem and my wife to get kidnapped," I yell and grab the bottle of water from the coffee table and take a huge gulp to calm down. I really thought all the bad things went away and now we were going to live happily ever after but—. Future is still in her wedding dress shocked as I am. Andrew tried to get her to change when we got to our house, but she wouldn't.

"I promise we are going to find them," the detective I learned his name is Bruce says.

"Forget it, I will find them myself. I don't want your help," I say.

"Why would David kidnap a kid though?" Nate asks. This is the first he has spoken since we found the blood. I have never seen him so speechless before and I realized that at that time I really needed him to crack one of his jokes.

"I don't know but when I find him, I will fucking kill him," Shawn says and sit on the couch. Dad took Nora and Kyle's mom home to rest.

"I know you are angry but let us help, you need us. You don't have a gun," Bruce points out.

"Fine but we are doing it my way," Bruce nods.

A phone ringing has our heads turning and Andrew hands me my phone.

"It's a video call," he informs.

I accept and Kyle tied to a chair appears on the screen.

"Hi, little nephew!" David's voice rings in my ears.

"What do you want with my son you asshole?" Shawn spit.

"Ah! You are the father. A little birdie told me that little Kyle has a heart condition, and it is just tragic that he doesn't have his medication. Don't worry I will send you his body, I am not that cruel,"

"You little—"

"Save the insults. I am not done yet," he laughs, and I feel sick to my stomach.

"You see Tay, you made a big mistake helping that bitch Emily and taking my company away from me," David says.

"Where is Olivia?" I ask.

"I can't wait to see your face when you see this," he shifts the camera and Olivia comes to the screen with a gun to her head.

"Hello old friend," a familiar says.

"Chad?"

"I go by Silas. Your whole fucking family ruined my fucking life and I'm going to make sure you feel what I felt all these years. Hey there little bro, Andrew."

CHAPTER 27

OLIVIA

"You fucked up my life," David says in my face.

"Because of your existence and the ability to attract men ruined my life!" He yells in anger at my face, and I flinch.

"I didn't ruin your life you psycho," I yell back with a pounding heart.

"You don't know how much I want to strangle you to death, but I was ordered not to touch a single hair on your body. The luck you have!" He chuckles and my heart sinks.

"You were ordered!"

"By Chad?"

"By his dick. Idiot."

Chad or Silas whatever the fuck his name is walks in.

"W... what the hell is this?" I demand and glare at him.

"I am going to tell you a story," he grabs a chair at the corner and sets it in front of me and sits down.

"There was this boy who loved his mother so much that he would do anything to see a smile on her face. He didn't have a father, you know why?" He looks at me.

"No, why?" I am not sure if I want to know the answer.

"Because he killed his own father. His father was a monster who used to beat the crap out of his mother. He used to sit in the corner every night of his little house and watched his mother get beaten to a pulp and one day he had enough and defended his mother. A part of him didn't want to kill him but he was too angry to control his anger or stop, so he stabbed his father over, and repeatedly until he was satisfied," he pushes his hair back.

"And instead of calling the police the son, grandmother and the mother covered a murder. Well, the mother and grandmother and the little one just watched them burying the body from a window," he chuckles.

"The little guy didn't feel anything and from that, he made a vow to protect his mother for the rest of his life, but he failed because his mother was murdered, and he wasn't there to prevent it. He became an Orphan," a tear falls from his eye.

"Do you know what it feels to become an Orphan? To have someone be taken from you?" he asks, and I shake my head no.

"The grandmother and the boy changed their identities and the boy started to call his granny his mother. They made sure not to leave any clue behind and the boy started to plot, to avenge his mother's death." He says and my heart pounds against my chest.

"You are him," I whisper with tears falling down my cheekbone.

"Say it," he demands, and I shake my head no.

"SAY IT OLIVIA?" he yells, and I close my eyes.

"You are Andrew's half-brother," I say and sob.

"Yes, I am." He pushes his chair back and stands up.

"Why did you kidnap us?" I ask and look up to him, and the man my eyes see is not the man I knew. The man standing in front of eyes is cruel, scary, and a psychopath.

"Kyle was the only way for you to come to me. I only want you." He informs and my eyes widen.

"What do you want from me?"

"You," He brings his hand to my face, and before he can touch it, I turn my head to the other side.

"I wanted you, I still do. We would have been happy together, but you had to choose him! I tried to separate you, but you always go back to him. I gave you a job, killed his mother, and sent that video of Donald and you all over but you still went back to him. Why?" He informs and my eyes water at the new information.

"You killed his mother!"

"Oh no! My hands are clean and besides I did her a favour. She was going to die. You know sometimes the people that stab you in the back are the ones closest to you. A few thousand was enough to have a maid finish her off," he chuckles with a smirk.

"I made sure the video went viral, but you still went back! This—" he points around us.

"Wouldn't have happened if you just came with me. I would have forgotten my plans to avenge my mother. I would have forgotten that the Payne's caused my grandmother to have Alzheimer's because of the loss of her only daughter. They also took her away from me, the Payne's took everything from me, and I will make sure they pay," he roars.

"The person who did it is dead, "

"Not enough. I will make sure every one of them suffers, starting with Tay."

"Okay, this is getting boring now," David says.

"You got what you wanted, now give me the money you promised to get me out of the country," I don't have time to react when Chad turns around grabbing his gun from the back of jeans and shot David right on the forehead causing me to scream

"Good riddance to bad rubbish," he blows the smoke coming from the bullet hole and I scream more.

CHAPTER 28

OLIVIA

"Open your eyes little one," Chad says to my face but I keep my eyes closed. He is a psychopath. How can he kill someone so easily! I have never in my life seen anyone die in front of me and what I just witnessed was pure horror! I don't know if I will ever get the image out of my mind.

"Open your eyes, Olivia?" I shake my head no while tears stream down my cheekbones. I am scared to open my eyes because then it will all be true that he killed David. A part of me hopes that it is all in my mind, that he didn't just put a bullet in David's skull right in front of my eyes. I feel a gun on my head and my breath hitches in my throat.

"Open your fucking eyes, Olivia?"

"Please don't shoot me!" I beg, my eyes still closed.

"I won't if you open your eyes," I slowly open my eyes to face the monster of every child's dream. David's body on the floor with blood around him. I feel like puking.

"Good girl!" He tucks my hair behind my ear.

"If only you returned my love for you, none of this wouldn't be happening," he leans against the wall in my sight.

"You don't have to do this Chad? I know you are hurt and feel like the whole world is against you but it's not," he keeps quiet, and I continue.

"You can still have the life you dreamt of if you only just drop this and move on. Don't let the anger you are feeling right now turn you into something you are not. There is someone out there that can love you," I try to reason, and he walks towards me.

"Can you?" His thumb caresses my cheek and I try not to show how much I hate him right now. How much I want to remove his hands off my face.

"Can you love me?" His voice is vulnerable, and I realize at that moment how life has been unfair to him. He watched his mother get beaten by his father every single night, watched his mother and grandmother bury his father, his mother got murdered and his grandmother also died. He is all alone in this world, and he is trying to hurt everyone who played a role in his misery.

"You can teach me," I swallow the lump that has formed on my throat. I don't why I said that, but it just came out. A part of me hopes he believes me and lets me go. He leans in to try to kiss me, but I turn my head at the last second.

"Lies!" He yells and kicks the chair next to him causing me to flinch.

"All you do is lie. I hate liars and you just lied to me, Olivia?" He looks madder than the last time.

"I had everything planned from the beginning, way before you came into the picture." He starts.

"Ria," he laughs, and my eyes bulge out of their socket.

"She was easy to manipulate, easy to get her to sleep with Tay while giving me information about his life," more tears fell down my cheeks as he revealed more information.

"David, poor David! The man was stupid I tell you," He laughs again while rubbing the gun against his head like a mad person.

"He was willing to screw his family over a few millions. I almost forgot the part where I enjoyed watching Tay search for the money that didn't even know where it went when it was right under his nose."

"What do you mean?" I manage to ask.

"I transferred the money to his dearest father. No, I'm lying. I set him up." He confesses and my heart is beating so fast I don't think I will handle any more of his bomb.

His phone beeps and he takes it out. A smile breaks on his face.

"Looks like dearest husband has come to rescue," he tucks his phone back to his jeans pocket. Tay is here!

"Okay, you have—" he checks his wristwatch.

"20 minutes to decide whether you are coming with me or you die," he drops another bomb.

"You are going to kill me!"

"Me? No. But your husband will. Believe me on that, "

"So, what is your decision?"

"I am not going anywhere with you," I say my heart pounding against my chest. There is no way in hell I am leaving with him. I would rather die.

Twenty minutes later, I am tired to a chair, my mouth covered and a wire from my chair going behind the door tied to a gun pointing at me. The door is closed and if anyone opens it the gun will go off. Gun shoot rings in my ears and all I hope for is for Tay or anyone not to open the door even though I know that is lightly never going to happen.

"Olivia?" A voice that can turn me on at any moment yells in the building but no matter how much I try to get free, I can't.

"Olivia? If you can hear me, please give me something, anything?" Tay's desperate voice rings in my ears and I struggle against the chair. His voice gets closer and closer and my heart beats faster and faster.

The doorknob turns and Tay's face comes into view. My eyes stay glued to the gun that is close to going off hoping he will see it and close the door but instead, he opens the door wider rushing to me and the gun goes off.

CHAPTER 29

TAY

Everything in me felt like it was burning, like my insides were burning at the sight of Olivia's unconscious body in my arms. I don't even know if she is unconscious or dead.

"Tay let the paramedics help her?" a voice says but it sounds too far away. The only thing in my mind right now is Olivia. I don't know how long I have been holding her, I just don't want her to slip out of my hands. It feels like the moment she does I will never see her again and that scares the shit out of me.

"Come, brother," two arms grab me, and Olivia gets taken away from me.

"She is in safe hands," a voice says, and we walk out of the building. I get at the back of the ambulance with Olivia and paramedics.

"Female, she looks like she is in her early twenties, one gunshot to the torso, and lost a lot of blood," a guy tells someone at the other side of the phone, and I continue to hold Olivia's hand.

"Yes, she is in critical condition," the guy keeps talking and I try my best not to snap at him. I am doing my best not to panic and all he is doing is making me worry more.

If only I had not opened that damn door, maybe she would be in my arms going home with me right now. Why is the universe so hell-bent on punishing me? All I want is to be happy with the woman I adore. I can still hear the gunshot going off in my mind. One ended up in Olivia's body. I am frightened and my soul feels like it is slowly slipping away from my body. I don't know if I can survive if she doesn't make it, she is a part of me, and without her, I have nothing to live for. Losing her will be like living in a world without air and I don't want to know how it feels.

The ambulance comes to a halt, and they wheel Olivia inside the hospital. Nate, Andrew, Jessica, Joe, Nora, Shawn, and I rush behind.

We sit in the waiting room and wait.

After many hours of waiting, James comes out and we all stand up.

"How is she?" I ask, not sure if I want to know the answer.

"We managed to remove the bullet," he informs and we all sigh.

"Will she be fine?" Nate asks.

"About that," he clears his throat.

"We had to put her in a coma for them to survive or else she won't make it to tomorrow an-"

"Them? Who are they?" I ask, confused?

"You didn't know?"

"Know what?" I ask, more confused.

"Olivia is pregnant with twins and it is a miracle that they all survived," my heart beats faster than normal. I open my mouth to say something but close it again. I don't know how to feel right now. I am happy and sad at the same time.

"Olivia is pregnant?" I ask, again just be sure I heard him right.

"Yes, she is 4 weeks pregnant," he informs.

"And why do you need to put her into a coma again?" I ask.

"She needs to heal, she took a bullet, and for the babies she has to be in a coma," James says and we all nod in understanding.

I sign some papers and later James allows me to go see her. There is a big tube going into her mouth and many small tubes on her arms and it takes everything in me not to break down and cry. I sit next to her bed and hold her hand.

"We are pregnant, you are going to be a mother and you will live to see our babies grow up, I promise my love. Just fight. I am waiting for you, I love you so much it hurts, and I love every minute of it."

CHAPTER 30

TAY

1 month later.

One month has passed and nothing has changed. Olivia is still the same, in a coma. She is not showing yet and I have spent every day with her, day in and night. Sometimes I forget what day it is. I have tried everything I have read online to try to get her to wake up, but nothing worked so far. James said she will wake up when she is ready which frustrates me because I am longing for that beautiful smile of hers. One month without her feels like a nightmare straight from a movie. All I do is shower and come back to the hospital. Our house in Cape Town is busy getting built and I know she will be happy with it when she wakes up.

Nate got an apartment with Rachel a few days ago. As much as I wanted to be happy for him, my mind is somewhere else. Andrew and Future are also doing well, and Eric is turning out to be a good boy. Nora is a mess like me. She also spends most of her days here with me. Olivia is like a daughter to her, and she is afraid of losing her like she lost Grace. Joe is trying to be strong for the both of them, but you can see that he is also suffering without his bundle of joy.

As for Chad, they didn't catch him. As much as I would like to hate him, I don't because life has been unfair to him. He went through so much at such a young age and my mother played a huge role in it too. Andrew didn't want to hear anything about Chad, we all tried to get him to talk to us, but he refused. Sometimes it's true when they say children pay for their parent's mistakes, and we all did, especially me, and I don't want my kids to suffer for my mistakes like I did.

"Go home and get some rest, honey? I will stay with her," a voice says breaking me from my heavy thoughts. I turn to look at Nora and shake my head no, even though I feel tired.

"Olivia won't like this, please go home and get proper sleep? You have spent the last two days here. I promise that I will call if anything changes," Nora says grabbing my arm and I stand up rubbing my eyes.

"Okay, " I hug her.

"Get a cab. You are too tired to drive," I kiss her cheek and walk out.

I run my hand through my hair and walk to the exit. I hail a cab and give the driver my address.

Half an hour later, the cab stops in front of my house, and I pay the driver and climb out. I walk inside the house and head straight to our room. Her scent has faded, and I have nothing to comfort me anymore. I sigh and walk to the bathroom, strip out of my clothes and step into the shower. The hot water relaxes my tense muscles as I wash my hair.

Half an hour later, I step out of the shower and wrap a towel around my waist and grab another one to dry my hair.

I dress up in grey track pants and continue to dry my hair. I throw the towel on the bed and walk out of the room barefooted and into the kitchen. I open the fridge and take out a small Tupperware of lasagne and place it in the microwave to heat it up. I pour myself an orange juice and sit on the barstool waiting for my meal.

Two minutes later, I take it and start eating. The house is quiet, and this is the worst feeling ever. I have been sleeping alone and eating alone.

I finish eating at the same the front door opens and Rachel and Nate holding a box walk in. He places the box on the kitchen counter.

"Hey, how is she?" He asks and sits on the barstool.

"Same as last month, what is inside the box?" I ask and gulp down the rest of my juice.

"It's Olivia's sequel for Behind Closed doors," Rachel informs me and I pull the box close to me.

"Sequel? I didn't even know she was writing it!" I open the box.

"She was, she gave me the last chapters weeks back." Rachel informs and I grab a copy. The cover is her on an open road with her arms crossed over her chest, her hair down.

"All roads lead to love," I read the title.

"Catchy title," Nate comments, and I nod with a proud smile on my face. I go to the last page to see how it ends.

I am his and he is mine, and in the end, it was him and I! No matter what road life leads you to, it always ends up to love. Your Tay is out there waiting for you, just like I found mine! I read and my heart does a backflip.

"She wrote about us!" My mind is racing, and I am not sure if I want to read it, afraid to read all the horrible things I said and did to her.

"She sure did!" Rachel chuckles.

"I am more in love with sister-in-law every day, she sure knows how to get payback!" I glare at Nate, and he grabs the book from my hands.

"When is it coming out?" I ask, taking out more books.

"Next week," I nod.

"Close the door when you guys leave, I'm going to bed," I say and Nate nods. I walk up the stairs and make my way to our room. I lay on the bed with my right arm behind my head and the left one on my stomach and watch the ceiling until my eyes burn to sleep.

CHAPTER 31

NATE

5 months later,

I have always been the relaxed one in the family and now was the time to make everyone smile. Ever since sister-in-law has been in a coma, I haven't seen Tay smile or laugh. 5 months have passed, and my brother looks like a living zombie. If he isn't in the hospital, he is drowning himself in work and I am afraid he will go back to his old self if sister-in-law doesn't wake up. Even though I miss her smile, I miss messing with her too.

"Where the hell are you taking me?" Tay groans as I continue to drag him.

"It's a surprise," I say and open the door to the spare room.

"Surprise!" Andrew, Future, Rachel, and little Eric who doesn't even have a clue what is going on cheer.

"What's going on?" Tay asks, looking around the empty room and six buckets of paint on the floor.

"We thought it would be fun if we painted a room for the twins. Since we don't know the genders yet, we bought white," I explained and waited.

"Of course, if you don't want—" he cuts off my rambling by pulling me into a hug.

"Thank you," he says with a weak smile on his face.

"Yeah, but it wasn't entirely me and—"

"Nate?" Tay says and I look at him.

"Yeah?" I finally breathe.

"Shut up," he laughs for the first time in 5 months, and I zip my mouth using my hands.

We open the buckets and mix the paint. I press play on the small radio I brought and Tequila by Dan + Shay roars in the room.

"Seriously!" Andrew says and I laugh.

"When I taste tequila!" I sing with a bright smile on my face, and everyone laughs at my childish act and that's what I always wanted to see in the past 5 months.

For the next two hours, we paint and make jokes. I know soon reality will set in but for now I am enjoying this little moment, the memories we are making. I dig my hand in the bucket of paint and paint Rachel on the face. Her mouth opens in disbelief, and I laugh at her clenching on my stomach. I predict her move and drop down on the floor and Tay gets the end of it causing me to laugh my ass off with tears streaming down my face.

"I am so sorry. I swear I didn't mean—" Rachel tries to explain and I feel liquid on my head and my eyes widen. Tay is holding an empty bucket with a smirk on his face.

"You didn't!" I say even though I know the answer to my question. White paint creates a curtain on my face, and I wipe it off standing up.

"You are so dead!" I threaten and run towards him, but I slip on the paint and fall.

"That deserved to be filmed," Andrew says laughing.

"Oh my God! Are you okay?" Rachel asks, hovering above me with a smile on her face. She offers me her hand and I take it but instead of standing up I pull her down and she screams. Seconds later, a paint fight breaks out.

A phone rings and we stop what we were doing, and watch Tay answer his phone with a smile on his face.

"Hello?" He says and seconds later, his smile drops.

"Did something happen? Is Olivia okay?" He asks standing up and we follow him.

"Okay, I am coming," he hangs up and before we can ask him what's wrong, he is out the door.

"Tay?" I call after and he continues to walk to his room

"What happened? Tay?"

"What the hell do you want Nate? Because of you, I wasn't there for Olivia. Do you think this is the time to have fun? No! So please leave me the fuck alone," he snaps panting and I shut my mouth.

"I'm sorry, okay? It's not your fault," he pulls me into a brief hug and walks into his room.

TAY

I step out of the shower and dry myself. I dress up in grey jeans with a long sleeve white t-shirt and a black cotton jacket. I grab my car keys and walk out. I find everyone in the kitchen all cleaned up.

"We are coming with you," Nate says standing up and we all walk out.

I go with Nate and Rachel and Andrew goes with Future in his car.

I should have been in the hospital with her but instead, I was having fun. What kind of a husband does that make me? When Nora said something happened to Olivia my heart stopped for a second.

Half an hour later, I park in the hospital lot, and we all climb out and rush inside.

We find Joe and Nora waiting in the waiting room.

"Has James said anything?" As if on cue he walks out, and we rush to him.

"What is going on?" I ask James and he looks at me then the others.

"Can I talk to you, Nora and Joe in private?" He asks and I nod. We follow him to his office.

"James, what's going on?" Nora asks this time.

"Tay you know Olivia can't carry a baby full tenure, right?" He asks and I nod with a pounding heart. I totally forgot about that.

"The pregnancy is taking a toll on her. She is not recovering the way we thought she would," he informs us.

"What does that mean?" Joe asks.

"It means you have to make a decision," he clears his throat and shifts in his chair.

"What kind of a decision?" I ask, not sure if I want to know the answer.

"To save the babies or Olivia during birth," he says and everything spins.

"Save her of course," Joe says, and James and Nora turn to me.

"What are the chances that she will survive?" I ask with a lump in my throat.

"10 percent," he says, and I wipe my sweaty hands against my jeans.

"Do everything you can to save all three of them, "I inform James.

"What! No," Joe pushes his chair back and stands up.

"I am not letting you save your children and let my only daughter die. Save my daughter James, I don't care if the twins die. She can always make another baby." he yells.

"Uhm, I cannot do that Joe. You have no right to decide on this one. I called you in because you are Olivia's father, and you deserve to know what's going on. They are Tay's children and Olivia is his wife, I'm sorry. And if Olivia manages to survive along with the twins, she will never be able to get pregnant again because of her condition," James explains and Joe storms out and Nora follows him.

"Would you like to know the gender?" James asks after a while, and I nod.

I follow him to a room and find Olivia already in it. I sit by her side and hold her hand. How much I wish she was awake and see our babies. James applies something on Olivia's belly and seconds later I hear heartbeats.

There they are, my beautiful babies.

James explains to me what's going on the screen, and I hold Olivia's hand all the time.

"Are you ready for the gender?" He asks and I nod. He hands me a picture and I take it.

"You guys are having a girl and a boy,"

CHAPTER 32

TAY

7 months later.

7 months have passed, and Olivia is still in a coma. I might be sad that she is still in a coma, but I am proud of her and her work. Her book has hit the top-selling books and she is on the list of bestselling author and now people in other countries know her and her series too. I just wish she would wake up and see the success of her books. Her fans are wishing her a good recovery and it still amazes me every time I read their messages. I have spent the last 3 months reading All roads lead to love for Olivia and playing audios of her to our twins hoping that they will at least hear their mother's voice.

Nora and I went to get baby shopping for the twins a few weeks back since we got to know the gender. Joe is still not keen on me choosing all three of them to be saved and he doesn't talk to me much anymore. James has been monitoring Olivia for the past months and has warned us that something can go wrong anytime, and they would have to operate so we have to be ready for anything.

Our house in Cape Town is finished and I haven't had the time to fly and see it. A part of me didn't want to see it alone so I decided to wait for Olivia and the twins. Emily has come back into town because David is dead and is tired of hiding. She and James have gotten close and although they are not dating it is bound to happen anytime soon. Jessica decided to pursue her career of being a detective and she has replaced Oliver. Little Kyle has a new heart and is a happy young man. Nate is now a big star in the sports world. The best player and captain of the Wolves. He has been traveling all around the world for the past three months and I am proud of him for achieving so much at such a young age like Olivia. Rachel's publishing company is also now a big thing, the identity reveal of Olivia really put the company's name out there. The most surprising thing was when my Instagram followers increased like a waterfall. I already had millions of followers but now they reach about 500 million. I didn't handle my social media accounts but now I decided to handle it myself since most of the followers are Olivia's fans and want to see if I will post anything about her. I post pictures I managed to take of her when she was not looking every day.

Andrew and Future are doing well in their careers and little Eric is growing up to be strong. My father is still in jail along with Donald and I have never visited them once. My father tried to call me from jail, but I always declined the call. He is dead to me, and I don't want him anywhere close to the twins. So far everything has been going well for others except for me.

A knock on the door brings me out of my long train of thought and Rachel's head pops in.

"Can I talk to you for a second?" She asks and I look back at Olivia on the hospital bed and back at Rachel nodding my head. I place a kiss on her forehead and head to the door stretching out. I find Rachel pacing in the hallway holding a brown envelope.

"Are you okay?" I ask and push my hair off my face. A reminder that I need to have a haircut and if Olivia wakes up and sees my hair, she will probably have the scare of her life. I have never had long hair in my life. I always made sure to have a haircut every month but since Olivia has been in a coma, I haven't had a haircut and you can only imagine how long my hair is.

"Yes, I am fine. You must see this," she hands me the envelope and starts biting her nails. I look at her for a moment and open the envelope and take out the papers and read.

"This is a contract," I say, confused as to why she wants me to read a contract when she could take it to her lawyers.

"I know, just read where it is written what it is for," she says, and I sigh but read it.

"Film/Tv distribution production. SK studios offer to buy rights from Olivia Kat Payne's book series to turn into a movie series!" My eyes bulge out of their sockets and my heart feels like it's going to pop out of my chest.

"No way!" I say, not believing I just read that. Someone wants to turn Olivia's books into a movie series!

"I know! I couldn't believe it too but there it is. I thought SK studios were joking when they approached me with the idea but when I got the contract, I was speechless. I know the books have been doing well for the past months, mainly because Olivia has been in a coma, but I didn't think they would reach this level!" Rachel says and tucks her hair behind her ear.

"What now? " I ask.

"We wait for Olivia to wake up. There is nothing we can do, I already told them too. We cannot sign on Olivia's behalf. She must read the contract and if she likes their offer then she will sign," Rachel informs and I nod in understanding.

"This is insane!" I comment.

"It is," Rachel agrees and I place the contract back in the envelope and hand it back to her.

"You hold on to it," she suggests.

"Okay, "

"I have to go, let me know if anything changes?" I nod and she hugs me and walks to the exit. A lot of things have changed, and I no longer dislike Rachel for being part of the reason why my brother almost died. Olivia being in a coma brought all of us closer to each other.

I walk back to the room and sit next to Olivia's bed.

"Hey!" I touch her hand.

"I have great news for you," I smile and tuck her hair behind her ear.

"Your books are doing so well that SK studios want to turn them into a movie series!"

"You have to wake up. So many beautiful things are waiting for you!" I say and suddenly, a machine starts beeping continuously.

"Code blue. Room 4." A voice announces.

"Olivia?" I push my chair back and stand up at the same time the door opens and James and three nurses rush in.

"What's going on?" I ask but James ignores me.

"Her blood pressure is dropping," he tells the nurse next to him.

"James, what's going on?" I ask again and he ignores me yet again.

"We need to operate now, "

"JAMES!" I yell and he finally looks at me.

"Get him out of here!" he instructs the nurses.

"Wait, what!" The nurse drags me out and closes the door behind me.

"What happened?" Nora asks.

"I don't know, I was just talking to her now and all of a sudden the machine started beeping, "I explain. Nora back tracts and Joe helps her down. The door to Olivia's room opens and nurses and James walk out wheeling Olivia.

"James, what is going on?" Joe asks.

"We have to operate, and I promise I will do my best to save all three of them," with that he runs to the direction they wheeled Olivia to. I text everyone and wait with Nora and Joe.

Half an hour later, everyone is here except for Nate since he is in Australia, and it will take hours for him to get here. After hours of sleeping on the hospital chairs and lots of coffee James finally walks out of the theatre room.

"What happened? Are Olivia and the twins, Okay?" I ask, not sure if I want to know the answer.

"Yes," he says, and we all release breaths we didn't even know we were holding.

"The twins are premature so they will have to stay in the incubator for two months," he informs, and I nod in understanding.

"And Olivia?" Joe asks.

"She will be okay. We moved her to intensive care so that she can heal. Her body took a lot of strain, but she will be fine. We gave a sedative. She will be asleep for 48 hours." James informs us.

"Can I see the twins?" I ask, my heart beating faster than normal.

"Follow me," James says and Nora decides to go with me since only two can see them at a time. James makes us wear hospital gear with gloves and we follow him to the small room.

Two incubators greet us. They look so small.

"They look so small," Nora comments and James chuckles.

"Can I get close?" I ask and James nods. Their eyes are closed, and they are the perfect image of Olivia and me.

"Have you decided on names?" Nora asks and I nod touching the glass.

"Noah and Natasha." I tell Nora and turn to look at her.

"Olivia will love them, I do."

"Who is older?" I ask James.

"Noah."

CHAPTER 33

TAY

Two days have passed by as a blur and Olivia hasn't woken up, but I have a feeling she will soon. I have spent most of my time with the twins. Nate is back and now we are just waiting for Olivia to wake up. Everyone loves the twins, and I couldn't be any happier.

"She will wake up man," a voice says, and I turn my head in Nate's direction and nod. I continue to rub my thumb on her hand.

"I know," I say and yawn. I haven't gotten any proper sleep for the past 2 days and now it is taking a toll on me.

"I am going to get something to eat, do you want something?" Nate asks.

"Just coffee," he nods and walks out. I place my head on the small space on the bed and soon sleep takes over.

OLIVIA

My whole body hurts, that's the first thing I feel. I struggle to open my eyes but minutes later I manage to open them. I try to move up, but pain shoots me back down and I groan. I have no idea where I am, and I'm confused as hell. I look around the room and realization hit me that I am in a hospital, and I notice Tay sleeping with his head close to my hand. I pull his hair since I can't reach him fully.

"T—" I clear my throat.

"Tay?" I whisper and he groans but wakes up. He looks confused for a minute but when he sees me, he is on his feet in seconds.

"Oh my God! I can't believe you are awake. Do you want something? Are you comfortable enough? Are you in any pa—" I touch his arm and he finally breaths and looks at me?

"Calm down," I tell him, and he pushes his hair back and I notice how long his hair is. He could even do a ponytail if he wanted.

"Your hair....is long," I clear my throat again. Tay grabs a bottle of water and opens it and brings it to my mouth.

"Yeah, a haircut was the last thing on my mind," he says helping me drink the water.

"What happened? Why am I in a hospital?" I ask, trying to move again and wince in pain.

"Easy," Tay says and the door opens to reveal everyone chatting and when Nora looks at me, she halts with wide eyes.

"Oh my God!" Nate says and I frown at everyone's behaviour.

"Why do you guys look like you have seen a ghost?" I ask, truly confused.

"I can't believe this," Nora says walking towards me.

"Uhm!"

"I am glad you are awake?" Nora hugs me causing me to wince in pain.

"Sorry, it's just good to see you," Nora says with a smile on her face.

"I will go get a doctor," Andrew says and hands Nate a brown paper bag.

"It's good to see you, sister-in-law. I was starting to think you enjoyed being in a co....ah!" Nate glares at Tay for smacking the back of his head and I also look at him confused as to why he smacked Nate.

"What the hell man!" Nate rubs the back of his head. The door opens and James walks in with Andrew and dad behind him.

"Hey! How are you feeling?" James asks and comes to my side?

"Sore," I inform him, and he chuckles.

"Is to be expected. I will give you something for the pain but now I need you to answer some questions. Do you think you could do that for me?" He asks and I nod. I feel a thumb drawing circles on my hand and I already know who it is.

"Can you tell me what year it is?" James asks.

"2020," I reply.

"What is the last thing you remember?" He asks and I relax on the bed.

"I remember—" and just like that everything comes to me like a waterfall. My conversation with Chad, him shooting David in front of my eyes, his past, and gunshots.

"Chad—"

"I know," a voice says, and I turn to look at Tay and notice everyone is gone.

"It's okay, it will be fine," he wipes my tears off, but will it? Will I ever be able to get the image of David in his own pool of blood out of my head?

"How long have I been in the hospital?" I ask.

"7 months," Tay informs me, and my heart pounds against my chest.

"Was I hurt that bad?"

"Yes, but you were in a coma for something else too," Tay says.

"You were pregnant," he informs, and my breath hitches in my throat.

"I lost it didn't I?" I ask even though I already have the answer to my question.

"No, you didn't. You gave birth to beautiful twins. Do you want to meet them?" Tay asks with a bright smile on his face.

"I gave birth to twins! Are you sure? I mean the doctors said I would never be able to carry a baby full term, "

"I am sure," he chuckles and pushes a wheelchair close to my bed. I want to believe him; I really do but I find it hard to believe. He lifts me up from the bed and places me on the chair and he wheels me out of the room.

"I have proof also," Tay hands me his phone and I see pictures of me pregnant laying on a hospital bed and my heart beats so fast it feels like it's going to pop out of my chest.

"Oh my God!" He pushes the wheelchair through double doors. He puts gloves and a mask on my face and pushes me into a small room. Two incubators greet me.

"I may have forgotten to mention that we have a girl and a boy," he says, helping me to stand up.

"It's Noah and Natasha," he says, and I place my hand on the glass.

"They are beautiful!"

"They are so small," I comment, and Tay chuckles.

"Nora said the same thing when she first saw them too,
"

"I still can't believe this! I missed so much," I say with tears running down my cheeks.

"I made sure that I wrote everything down," Tay informs.

"What do you mean?"

"I bought a big journal and wrote everything about the pregnancy every day." He informs and I form a smile.

....

Days turn into months, and it was finally time to take the twins home. We decided to wait until the twins are old enough to travel to move to Cape Town. So much has happened in two months and I still can't believe it. I signed a contract with SK studios and my books are doing well. I have been going to therapy because of the trauma Chad did to me and my nightmares, it's going well.

Sometimes Tay goes with me. Everyone is doing great, and I don't have any complaints.

"How are they doing?" Tay asks and I look back at the backseat at the twins.

"They are asleep," I chuckle, and he pulls the car into our house's driveway. Everyone's cars are already parked. We decided to do a small brunch to celebrate life. I climb out of the car and open the backseat and take out Noah and Tay holds Natasha. We walk inside the house.

"Look who's back!" Nora rushes to us.

"They are asleep," I inform her, and she nods.

"Everyone is in the backyard. Food is ready," she kisses my forehead and heads out. Tay and I walk to the twin's room and place them in their crib. I grab the monitor with me, and we join the others in the backyard.

Loud cheers greet us, and I smile seeing everyone so happy. Nate is holding a beer talking to Andrew at the braai stand. They oversee braaing meat for us. Shawn is sitting with my father and James not far from the brothers also holding a beer. Kyle is playing with Eric. Emily, Future, and Jessica are setting the table.

"Guys! Food is ready," Nora yells and we all walk to the table. Nate places the tray of meat they braaied on the table.

We sit around the table and eat and laugh and it is the best feeling ever.

Hours later the baby monitor rings, and I excuse myself to check on the twins. I walk into the twins' room and find both of them awake.

"Hey, you two!" I say and the door opens and Tay walks in.

"I came to see if you needed any help?" He informs and wraps his arms around me from behind.

"We are fine," I smile, and he places a kiss on my shoulder.

"I love you,"

"I love you more,

Despite all those challenges life threw at us, we did it. We came out stronger than ever, together.

EPILOGUE

TAY

8 years later.

I massage my forehead as Jordan keeps talking, I have been in this meeting for an hour now and all I want is for it to end and catch a break. Running a company is no joke and I still have no fucking idea why I didn't hire a CEO and stay at home.

"The hotel in Limpopo needs…." A phone rings interrupts Jordan.

"I said no fucking phones in the board room!"

"Sir, it's yours." One speaks.

"Oh," I clear my throat and answer my phone.

"Yes?"

"Can I speak to Mr.Tay Payne?" a feminine voice requests.

"Speaking."

"This is the principle; your son was involved in a fight. I would like to discuss his behaviour with you."

"I will be there in 30 minutes." I hang up.

"Let me know what decision you guys reach, I have somewhere to be." I grab my car keys and walk out.

Noah has been acting out lately and I don't know what to do with him or what he is going through, is his adolescence stage at 8 years or what. Olivia babies him too much and I think that made him like this.

Ten minutes later I pull up in front of Rose Park Primary School and climb out of my Rolls Royce. The school is expensive as hell, and I have no idea how I agreed to pay so much money.

You made the promise when you were naked and in bed, my subconscious amuses me.

"Hi, I'm here to see the principal."

"Go in, they are waiting for you."

I knock and enter. Olivia is already inside with unfamiliar women, the principal and Noah and the kid he got in a fight with.

"Thank you for coming Mr. Payne. Have a sit."

"Noah has been getting into fights and today was the last straw. He locked Thabo in a storage!"

"He started it!"

"Shut up!" I say harshly to Noah.

"But dad…"

"Noah?" this time Olivia speaks.

"Now Noah is a bright kid but when intelligence is misused things end up getting out of control."

"You need to suspend him." The women speaks for the first time.

"Excuse me!" Olivia shouts.

"My child is traumatised by what your kid did!" the women I have no idea whose name is says.

"He started it." Noah yells at the women. Noah is short tempered and acts out when he is angry. He is like me and I'm afraid he will turn out to be like me and that's very bad.

"Thabo is what Noah saying true?" the principal enquires.

"No." Thabo.

"You are lying!" Noah pushes Thabo and he falls along with the chair.

"Noah!" we all say in union.

"He is lying mom!" Noah.

"Go take your sister and wait for us outside now!" he storms out.

"I'm so sorry about his behaviour. I will take talk to him I promise."

"He needs to be suspended," the women repeat.

"There's no need to do that," I say.

"I think a week off school will do him some good." Principal says.

"Thabo lets go." The women grabs her child and walk out.

"We will deal with Noah." I promise and we walk out.

Noah and Natasha are waiting for us next to Olivia's car and Noah is holding Nat's school bag.

"Get in the car," Olivia opens the back door for them, and I get in the driver's seat. I watch as Noah buckles Natasha's seat belt on and Olivia climbs in the passenger seat. I call my assistant to pick my car up.

"You are grounded. No phone, tablet, and TV." I tell Noah when I park in front of the house. He climbs out of the car and bangs the door and run inside.

"Was that necessary?" Olivia asks as we climb out.

"Go inside baby." Olivia tells Nat.

Nat follows Noah.

"You baby him too much."

"It won't hurt you to just sit down and talk to your son you know? You are always at work and when you are home you hardly spend time with him! He feels left out and that you love Nat more than him. Have you ever asked yourself why he is acting out?"

"I love them both equally."

"Show him," I sigh, and we walk inside, and I make my way to Noah's room. I knock and say, "Noah? It's me. Can I come in?" I wait and twist the doorknob and before I can act water gets splashed all over me.

"I hate you! Die!" Noah's voice screams and to say those four words hurt like a bitch will be an understatement. I never thought I would hear my own son say he hates me. I thought I was doing things right.

"What is going on?"

"Oh my God!"

"Noah!" I turn with a heavy heart and walk to our room. Have I been so bad that I made my son hate me? I don't want to be like my father or Olivia's father. I step into the shower with my thoughts racing and with no solution or answers for me. I can't figure where I went wrong with him.

I wrap a towel around waist and walk out to Natasha and Olivia talking.

"Please don't punish him? He did what he did to protect me. Thabo and his friends were bothering me and that's why Noah locked him in the storage." Olivia looks at me and the guilt is eating me up.

"Please mom?"

"We won't baby, okay?" Nat nods and runs out and I sit on the bed.

"Where did I go wrong with him?"

"He wants your attention. A few weeks off work and doing things with him will do the trick. He just needs you to be there at his games, do things together. You two share similarities I don't think it will be a problem to bond."

OLIVIA

I make sandwiches for the kids while they watch TV and I think of ways I can make Noah and Tay get along again. They are both stubborn and won't break so easily.

"Where are my little monsters!" Nate screams as he rushes in. He is the only one who calls my children monsters.

"Uncle Nate!" They run towards the voice and soon laughter fills the house.

"You need to stop calling my kids monsters," I say to Nate, and he laughs and says, "They are monsters. Have you seen them on full annoy Nate?" I shake my head and he tickles Noah on the couch and Tay walks into the lounge.

"Uncle stop!" I love seeing my kids laughing and happy. My phone rings and Rachel's name flashes on the screen. A reminder that her and Nate are getting married tomorrow. It took Nate 8 years to pop the question and we are proud of him. I'm happy he is getting married; it's about time.

"You two go pick up your bags." I say to the kid.

"Can you take Natasha with you only?" Tay requests.

"Okay."

"Noah, you are staying behind baby."

"Okay.' He says and goes back to what Nate was showing him.

"Are you okay?" I ask and wrap my arms around his neck.

"I will be when Noah stops hating me." I sigh and dig my fingers into his hair, and he moans.

"Don't stress too much we have a wedding tomorrow. Just do things with him." He nods and Natasha walks in with her back bag.

"I will see you tomorrow," I peck his lips and grab my car keys.

"Bye mom,"

"Bye baby."

At Rachel's house I find Future making snacks and Rachel in the living room.

"What's up bitches!"

"Where is that troublemaker of yours?" Future asks when she sees Natasha only.

"He stayed behind"

"Eric and Ana are upstairs." Future has a daughter two years younger than my twins.

We spend the rest of our hours complaining about our men, life and having a goodnight. Saluting the women who finally got Nate, one of the top 5 bachelors in South Africa to put a ring on it and putting our kids to sleep.

The next morning is a busy day with everyone getting ready.

"Where is Rachel?" I ask.

"I last spoke to her when she was taking a shower." Future informs.

"I will check up on her." I rush upstairs and walk into her room. I knock on her bathroom door and spot a paper on her bed. I walk to the bed and grab the letter and read.

"No, no, no." I run out of the room and the stairs.

"Olivia?" Future yells my name as I run out of the house. I climb into the driver's seat and speed to the church. Cars already parked in front of the church, and I make my way inside. Almost everyone is here as I walk to the brothers. Nate looks handsome in a tux and my heart breaks at the sight of him so happy.

"Olivia?" Tay says confused and rushes to me.

"Why are you here not dressed?" I ignore his question and hand Nate the letter.

"What's going on?" he asks taking the letter. The brothers watch Nate read the letter and after a while he stumbles back in shock dropping the letter and siting down.

"What is going on?" Tay asks grabbing the letter on the floor.

"Nate, I'm sorry for doing this to you again but I can't marry you when my heart belongs with someone else. I love Shawn and I hope you find someone who will love you like you deserve to be loved. I'm so sorry for doing this to you." Tay finishes reading and turns to Nate. He is just sitting on the floor, no reaction and none of us know what to say to him. What do you say to someone who has been left at the altar? He stands up and walks to the front doors.

"Nate?" Tay tries to stop him.

"I'm just going for a walk." His eyes are red, and he is doing everything he can not to break down this time. Tay lets him go and I'm sure we all wonder if he will recover from this.

THE END.

ACKNOWLEDGMENTS

I can't believe we have reached the end. Thank you to Grammar House, Graphicmart1, MFH Publishers, my parents and most importantly You. My readers. Thank you for going on this journey of Love, hate, laughs and passion with us. I hope these beautiful characters left you with something to remember them with.

Nate says, 'It's okay to hurt and cry. I don't believe time mend our wounds, we are bound to lose something or someone in this life but loving yourself, choosing yourself, and family is all we have and can do.'